OK, Jeopardy—" I started, but before I could say "over!" Jeopardy was gone. She leaped over that first hurdle and kept going. *Zip!* She went over the second hurdle. *Swish!* She flew over the third hurdle. "ARF ARF ARF ARF ARF!" she barked as she jumped.

"ARF ARF ARF ARF ARF ARF ARF ARF ARF!" She galloped in a huge circle around all of us, barking frantically.

"Jeopardy!" I shouted. I threw myself forward to grab her collar and missed. My chin hit the floor with a painful *thwack*.

Jeopardy stopped and stared at me from a few feet away.

"Come here!" I said.

"ARF!" Jeopardy answered and ran off with her tail wagging.

Get into some

Pet Trouble

Runaway Retriever

Loudest Beagle on the Block

Mud-Puddle Poodle

Bulldog Won't Budge

Oh No, Newf!

Smarty-Pants Sheltie

Bad to the Bone Boxer

Pet Trouble

Smarty-Pants Sheltie

by T. T. SUTHERLAND

SCHOLASTIC INC.

New York   Toronto   London   Auckland
Sydney   Mexico City   New Delhi   Hong Kong

ISBN 978-0-545-10303-9

12 11 10 9 8 7 6 5 4 3 2 1   10 11 12 13 14 15/0

Printed in the U.S.A.   40
First printing, March 2010

For Noah ☺

Pet Trouble

Smarty-Pants Sheltie

CHAPTER 1

My dog was staring at me again.

I have no idea what she wants when she does that. She just sits there and . . . stares. Her black eyes are kind of close together and she has this long elegant nose, and it's like she's peering down that nose at me, just . . . waiting for something. But I don't know what.

I wasn't even doing anything interesting. I'd unpacked a bag full of T-shirts and shorts and stuffed them into a couple of drawers, so I was sitting on my bed, taking a break from unpacking. I could see the corner of a red shirt sticking out of the drawer, but I didn't feel like getting up to fix it. My new room was still a disaster. It would take me weeks to make it look right. And my dog was sitting in the middle of the new rug, staring at me.

"Stop it, Jeopardy," I said.

She tilted her head as if I had said something

mysterious and fascinating. Her ears always stick straight up. It's like she's listening *really hard* even if nothing is happening at all. Her eyes went from my face to my hands to my face to my hands.

"I'm not doing anything!" I said. I held up my empty hands and she instantly jumped to her paws, wagging her tail. "Good grief, Jeopardy," I said. "Chill out."

I got up to get another box and she hurried over to nose at my hands and paw at the cardboard flaps. This had been happening all day. Every time I twitched or shifted, even a tiny bit, she'd jump to her paws as if I'd set off a burglar alarm. I couldn't move an inch without her following me across the room. Then she'd stare at me while I put something else away.

It made me nervous. How was I supposed to unpack with this dog fidgeting around and watching me like I was trying to hide the *Mona Lisa* or something?

"Mom!" I called. I wondered if Mom could hear me in this big old house. Our house in Rochester was just the right size for the four of us, but this new house had too many extra rooms, plus an attic and a basement. We didn't even have enough stuff to put something in every room. Mom said I could have the whole basement to hang out in if I wanted. But what good was a whole basement when I didn't have any friends to hang out *with*?

"Mom!" I called again, but there was no answer. I could hear clattering from the kitchen downstairs, so she was probably unpacking pots with my sister, Violet. Violet can usually drown me out, even without the help of her favorite pot lids. She's three and she is already the loudest person I've ever met.

I looked inside the box and sighed. I thought I'd hated packing, but it turned out *un*packing was even worse. On our last day in Rochester, when I couldn't put it off anymore, I had just started throwing all my stuff into any box I could find. So now I kept opening boxes packed like this: two yo-yos (one broken), nineteen Hot Wheels race cars, three paperback Hardy Boys books, a snow globe with the Eiffel Tower inside it from our trip to Paris, a set of military-looking dog tags with my name on them (which my friend Victor got for me for my eleventh birthday), a picture of me and Josh and our dads at a Buffalo Bills game, a deflated football, a couple of test tubes from the old chemistry set I lost a while ago, the mask and cape from my Zorro costume last Halloween, a watercolor painting of a horse that Anjali had given me to remember her by, the CD case for my favorite computer game (I had no idea where the CD itself was), and a Far Side wall calendar that was supposedly a Christmas gift from Violet, although of course it was really from my mom and dad, because, like I said, she's *three*. If she'd been allowed to pick out her own gift for me, I'd have ended up with, like, a purple stuffed hippo. Or a tutu. Or a pot lid, if I was really lucky.

What the heck was I supposed to do with all of this? I put the dog tags around my neck and looked at the inscription again: CAPT. NOAH LOCKE, BEST FRIEND SQUADRON. Victor's said SGT. VICTOR HALE, because he'd thought sergeants were above captains, so then it was really funny when we checked online and he turned out to be wrong.

I picked up the wall calendar and went looking for a thumbtack, but of course I couldn't find one. I couldn't find *anything* I actually wanted. I found a stapler and an orange highlighter in a box labeled DESK STUFF, but everything else in that box was old papers and homework assignments. I'd probably just emptied a whole drawer of my desk into the box and taped it up.

Man, I hated moving. When I get older, I'm going to find one perfect place to live (probably Rochester, if Victor and Todd and Anjali are still there) and never move again. I propped Anjali's horse painting on the windowsill, dug my laptop out of my backpack, and sat down on the floor. My old room had a fuzzy dandelion-yellow wall-to-wall carpet, but this new house had hardwood floors everywhere. Dad had found me a big orange-and-blue rug that covered most of the floor in my new room, but it was way less comfortable to sit on. I could tell I wouldn't be doing much homework on the floor anymore.

Jeopardy immediately came over and sat down next to me. I tried to ignore her while I turned the laptop on. But have you ever tried to ignore someone who's sitting a foot away from you, staring intently into your face?

"WHAT?" I finally said to her.

She tilted her head at me again.

"Can't you go bother someone else?" I asked.

She tilted her head the other way. When I didn't say anything else, she pawed at my knee with one delicate white paw.

Jeopardy is a Shetland sheepdog, or Sheltie for short. She looks like a small version of Lassie, with long brown- and white- and honey-colored fur. Her face is mostly honey-tan around her bright black eyes, with a small blaze of white across her nose. She has a halo of darker fur around that and dark brown ears, the same color as my hair (and, like me, she always seems to need a haircut). Her chest is a puff of white fur and all of her little paws are white.

She's really pretty, but I think she's really, really weird. We got her a year ago because my mom was on the TV show *Jeopardy!* and the dog was supposed to be a thank-you to the rest of us for helping her study before she went on. It surprised me because I never really thought about getting a dog. I guess we had a Dalmatian when I was really little, but I don't remember him much. Victor has a cat and Anjali has two chinchillas, so I'd thought maybe I'd get something like that one day.

But then my mom and dad came home with this fuzzy Sheltie puppy and decided to name her Jeopardy after the show. For no apparent reason, she loved me best of all. Even as a puppy, she'd kind of stagger around behind me, yipping until I picked her up. So first I had to get used to having a dog follow me around all the time. And then, six weeks ago, Mom and Dad told me we were moving.

Moving! Right in the middle of the school year! Well, kind of near the beginning, but my dad's job wouldn't let him move until October, so it meant that I'd have a month of sixth grade in Rochester, and then I had to start over here. What if they were studying different things? What if these sixth graders were way ahead of me?

But the worst part was leaving Victor and Anjali and Josh. I knew there wouldn't be anyone like them here. For one thing, I was pretty sure I was the only Buffalo Bills fan for three hundred miles.

And then there was Jeopardy. She'd always been a little crazy, but when we started packing she *totally freaked out*. She kept jumping into boxes while we were packing them, or grabbing whatever we were trying to pack and hiding it under the bed or in the sofa. She didn't let me out of her sight for the whole last week before we moved. She's supposed to sleep on the floor beside my bed, but I kept waking up in the middle of the night when she jumped up to sleep next to me.

I mean, I like my dog and all, but it was getting kind of annoying.

Speaking of annoying, we'd moved in on a Wednesday, and here it was already Saturday and we *still* didn't have an Internet connection. I was pretty sure someone was trying to torture me. All I wanted to do was e-mail my friends and make sure they still remembered me, but I couldn't even do that.

Jeopardy poked my elbow with her nose.

"*Stop it*," I said, frowning at her. "I'm not in the mood for your weirdness, Jeopardy."

Her ears perked up even more when I said her name. She stood up and wagged her tail as if *I'm not in the mood for your weirdness* actually meant *It's playtime!*

"MOM!" I yelled just as my mom appeared in the doorway.

"Goodness, Noah," Mom said. "There's no need to shout."

"YEAH, NOAH!" Violet hollered from behind her legs. "NO NEEDS FOR SHOUTING!"

Mom made that face where she's trying not to laugh. She thinks Violet is a lot funnier than I do. My sister and I both have blue eyes, but when Violet opens hers really wide and goes "What I do?" she can get away with anything. I guess the wispy blond ringlets probably help, too. Today she was wearing her sequined purple leotard backward, but she'd thrown a screaming fit when Mom tried to change it, so Mom just put a pink skirt over it and let her wear it like that. I was very sure I hadn't been that ridiculous when I was three.

"Mom, Jeopardy is driving me crazy," I said.

"Aw, come here, sweetie," Mom said to the dog, kneeling down. Her long, light brown hair was tied back with a thin blue scarf that had little gold spangles woven into it. Mom teaches high school, but sometimes she gets mistaken for one of the students because she looks really young. So whenever she's working, she wears jackets and heels and really professional-looking clothes (which is what she wore on *Jeopardy!* too). But today she was wearing jeans and a paint-spattered black T-shirt. The paint spots were lavender, the new color of Violet's walls (my sister has a thing for purple, if you're wondering).

Jeopardy trotted over to her, wagging her tail and ducking her head. She let Mom pat her for about ten seconds, and then she jumped away and looked at me again. Her golden-brown fur fluffed out around her face and her small black eyes were very serious.

"See?" I said. "It's like she wants me to do something. What do you want from my life, dog?"

Mom stood up and glanced around my room. I hadn't gotten much done since Wednesday. My orange-and-white-checkered bedspread was on my bed and half my clothes had made it into the closet. But there was nothing yet on the dark wooden bookshelf except a box of Kleenex, a framed photo of Josh and Anjali, and *Bridge to Terabithia*, which we read last year in fifth grade. There were open boxes stacked all over the room and piles of stuff that I couldn't deal with. The only thing on the wall was a collage of photos of African animals—another present from Anjali. I'd stuck it up over my bed on Thursday, using tape because I couldn't find anything else.

"Also," I said, "we still don't have the Internet, and I hate this floor."

"I HATES IT, TOO!" Violet bellowed. But she didn't mean it. She just repeats everything I say, because she's like Jeopardy in that she lives to annoy me.

Mom put her hands on her hips. "Maybe you need to go for a walk," she said to me.

Jeopardy's head whipped around at the word "walk." She stared at Mom, wagging her bushy tail frantically, *swish swish swish*.

"I don't want to go for a walk," I said.

Jeopardy nearly had a heart attack. She galloped over to me and tried to leap into my lap, which was already full of my laptop. She planted her front paws on my shoulders and poked her nose into my face with a searching gaze.

"ACK!" I yelled. "Quit it! Off!" I dove away from her and moved my laptop to the safety of the desk.

"There's a park only a few blocks away," Mom said firmly. "You can take Jeopardy. I think you both could use a break."

"That wouldn't be a break for me," I pointed out. "Since she'd still be there, staring at me. Like she *always does*." I widened my eyes at Jeopardy, but she just wagged her tail and stared back. I'd never beaten her in a staring contest.

"Should Violet and I come with you?" Mom asked.

"YES!" Violet shrieked.

"No!" I said. "Fine! I'm going!"

Mom had packed Jeopardy's stuff all in one box, so it was easy to find when we got here. Her silver chain-link leash was hanging on the front doorknob. As I went to put my sneakers on in the front hall, Jeopardy galloped over and grabbed her leash between her teeth. She pulled it off the door and dragged it over to me.

That's a new trick. We didn't teach it to her. In our old house, we kept her leash on a shelf next to the door, where neither Violet nor Jeopardy could reach it. But there wasn't a shelf like that here, so on Wednesday night after he walked her, Dad left it on the doorknob. Then on Thursday night, when he started getting ready to take her out, Jeopardy ran over and brought the leash to him. It didn't take her long at all to figure out where it was.

Violet, on the other hand, still hadn't found the downstairs bathroom.

I clipped the leash onto Jeopardy's new collar, which is pale green with dragonflies embroidered on it. I told Mom I thought it was too girly, but she said, "Well, Jeopardy *is* a girl," and I couldn't exactly argue with that.

The dog and I were already halfway down the block when I realized I had no idea where this "park" was. I was too annoyed to go back and ask Mom, so I let Jeopardy lead the way. I didn't care if we just went around the block and ended up at home again.

But Jeopardy had her own plans. She took me straight to the park. It's almost like she has a GPS in her nose or something. She kept stopping and looking back at me as if she couldn't understand why I was going so slowly. Or maybe she was checking to make sure I wasn't doing anything interesting while she had her eyes elsewhere.

It was already cold enough for a jacket in Rochester, but here I didn't need it yet. The sun was shining in this bright blue sky and the wind rustled through the trees so it sounded like the green and gold leaves were whispering about me. *Who's the new kid? He needs a haircut. Why's his dog so weird?*

Once we were inside the park, Jeopardy found the dog run in no time. It was a huge fenced-off area surrounded by thick hedges, with a water fountain in the middle and trees all around it. A little wooden post by the chain-link gate had a box of plastic bags attached to it and a sign that said: DON'T FORGET TO CLEAN UP AFTER YOUR DOG!

I was nervous as we walked up to the gate, but there wasn't anyone inside. That surprised me, because it was a Saturday morning, but I was glad, too. I took off Jeopardy's leash and headed for the dark green benches at the far end. I just wanted to sit and forget for a while about moving and unpacking and starting a new school in two days. I wasn't ready to talk to any strangers yet.

But it turned out I didn't have much choice. Five minutes later, Jeopardy barked and ran over to the gate. My heart sank as I saw a girl my age coming in with a giant shaggy dog.

Ready or not, I was about to meet somebody new.

CHAPTER 2

For a moment I thought about staying on my bench and hoping she wouldn't notice me, but Jeopardy was already leaping around the girl's feet and sniffing at the big dog. I wasn't sure if the girl would like that, so I had to go over and get my stupid dog to leave her alone.

"Sorry," I said, reaching for Jeopardy's collar, but the girl crouched down and started to pet her. Jeopardy poked her long thin nose under the girl's hand, and then backed away to focus on the other dog.

"That's OK!" the girl said to me. She smiled at Jeopardy in this big, excited way, like meeting a new dog was the highlight of her day or something. "What's your dog's name?"

"This is Jeopardy," I said. I wondered if she would think that was a weird name. I hoped I wouldn't have to tell the whole story of my mom being on the show and everything.

Her dog was absolutely enormous, with a huge black, shaggy head and gigantic white paws and really long black-and-white fur. His pink tongue hung out as he grinned at Jeopardy, who was darting around him like a mosquito, trying to get close enough to sniff him without getting swatted.

"I'm Noah," I added.

"Hi Noah," she said, shaking my hand. "I'm Heidi, and this is Yeti."

OK. I felt a little better. Yeti was at least as funny a name as Jeopardy, although it was pretty appropriate for such a big-pawed, Abominable-Snowman–looking dog.

Heidi was really tall, taller than me, with tangled blondish-reddish hair that looked like maybe she hadn't had time to brush it yet that morning. Her long-sleeved dark red shirt had a cartoon English sheepdog on the front and little white paw prints around the hem and collar and sleeves. There was a small chocolate stain on her left elbow, which puzzled me. How do you get chocolate on your *elbow*?

She kept touching her dog like she was making sure he was still there, although at that size he'd be pretty hard to miss. Yeti was tall enough that she didn't have to reach down to pat his head, and he kept leaning into her side with this adoring look on his face.

Jeopardy doesn't look at me like that. Her look is more like, *Well? What are we doing now? How about now? Really, we're still playing this video game? Still? How about now?*

"Do you live around here?" Heidi asked, holding her hand out for Yeti to lick her fingers.

"Yeah," I said. "I think so. I hope I can get home again." I realized how dumb that sounded when she started laughing. Man, I must have seemed like such a moron. *Way to make a good first impression, Noah.* By the time I got to school on Monday she would probably have told everyone how brain-dead I was.

Heidi stopped laughing and covered her mouth, looking worried. "Don't you know where you live?" she asked.

Sure I do. I live in Rochester, next door to Victor and across the street from Anjali and Josh. That's where I'm supposed to be right now.

"We just moved here," I said. I kicked a piece of gravel with my sneaker and Jeopardy pounced on it as it bounced away. "I start school on Monday."

"Really?" she said. Her blue eyes went really wide, kind of like Violet's when she's confused (or pretending to be confused). "But school started already!"

"I know," I said. *Tell me about it. Like I'm not worried enough.* It wasn't just the schoolwork that worried me. Everyone would already know where they were sitting at lunch. Everyone would have their best friends all set already. They'd know where everything was and who was cool and who wasn't and everybody's names and all this stuff it would take me forever to figure out. I was definitely not looking forward to Monday.

"Well, you didn't miss anything important," Heidi said, rolling her eyes. "Blah blah pyramids and South American geography and whatever."

Uh-oh. What exactly about pyramids and South American geography? We'd been doing Greek myths and long division back at my old school. I knew some South American geography, like the capitals of the countries, but nothing about, like, rivers or the tallest mountain or anything like that. Would I have to know all that stuff?

"Hey, maybe you'll be in my class," Heidi barreled on. She didn't seem to notice that she was freaking me out a little bit. "Sixth grade? Westminster Elementary?"

I nodded. "Mr. Perry, I think."

"Peary," she said, and I felt like an idiot again. Boy, getting the teacher's name wrong would be a terrific way to start off at my new school, wouldn't it?

"Oh, hey!" Heidi went on, her face lighting up. "That *is* my class! That's so cool! Mr. Peary is awesome!" She clapped her hands and bounced up and down. Her dog went "WOOF! WOOF!" and leaped up to plant his paws on her shoulders, and then Jeopardy got excited and tried to jump on her, too, and all three of them fell over in a big pile on the grass.

"Eeeee!" Heidi yelped as Jeopardy and Yeti both tried to lick her face. I jumped forward and grabbed Jeopardy's collar to pull her off. It figured my dog would do something totally embarrassing to the first person I met here.

"Are you OK?" I asked.

But Heidi was laughing like crazy. She couldn't stop laughing for a full minute, which was kind of funny and kind of odd at the same time. I wondered if maybe she was a little cuckoo herself.

Finally she sat up and gave her dog a hug. He nuzzled his nose into her neck. His head was literally bigger than hers. His big furry ears flapped as he panted and blinked at me.

"Yeah, I'm all right," Heidi said, catching her breath. She reached to pat Jeopardy's head, but Jeopardy ducked away and came over to sit next to me when I crouched down. I could sense the Sheltie staring at me out of the corner of my eye.

"Your dog is enormous," I said, which wasn't exactly brilliant conversation, but I couldn't think of what else to say.

"Isn't he huge?" she said, grinning. "Did you move here from Buffalo?"

I was confused for a minute, until I looked down and realized I was wearing one of my Buffalo Bills shirts. I hoped my dad didn't think we were going to change our football loyalties just because we lived somewhere new. I would always be a Bills fan, no matter where we lived, and no matter how often they lost. They were still the best football team ever, according to me and Josh.

"Rochester," I said, answering her question. "Close enough." Close enough to go to at least one Bills game a month, especially when Josh's dad had season tickets. But now we weren't close to Buffalo at all. I probably wouldn't get to go to another Bills game for the rest of the season. I missed it already—the stadium, the smell of the pretzels, huddling in our coats and blankets while the team played through a blizzard, arguing with Josh over who should be starting quarterback as Dad drove us home in the dark.

"You'll like it here," Heidi said, as if she'd read my mind. "There are lots of kids with dogs." OK, so she hadn't read my mind. I had enough trouble dealing with weirdo Jeopardy; I was pretty sure I'd be just as bad with other people's dogs. And if they saw how weird my dog was, they probably wouldn't want to be friends with me anyway.

"Some of my friends are coming now," Heidi said, sounding excited. She checked her wrist, although there wasn't a watch on it. "Um, sometime soon, anyway. You can meet them and all their dogs, too."

Oh, man. I was *definitely* not ready for a whole bunch of strangers and dogs. I wasn't sure I'd ever be ready. Unfortunately, Monday was coming no matter what I did. At least I could avoid the meeting-people part for a little while longer, though.

"Um, actually, I gotta go home," I said. I got to my feet and brushed dirt off my jeans. Heidi had smudges of grass and dirt on her knees from rolling around with the dogs. "I still have to unpack," I added. "My room is a mess." That was true, anyhow.

"Oh, please," she said, waving her hands around. "I am the queen of messy rooms. Are you sure you can't stay?"

"Sorry," I said. I grabbed Jeopardy and clipped her leash back on. My dog gave me this look like, *Really? Already? What if I want to stay? Can I stay and you go?*

Heidi looked pretty disappointed, too. I felt bad, but it was too late to be like, "OK, never mind, I'll stay," right? And even though she was nice, what if her friends weren't? Or what if they thought it was weird that I was hanging out with a girl? What if they tried to pat Jeopardy and she ran away from them and they decided that I was a bad dog owner?

No, it would be hard enough to meet people; I didn't need Jeopardy there making me look even dopier than usual.

"But, uh, it was nice to meet you," I said to Heidi.

"Nice to meet you, too," she said. "Good luck finding your way home!" I winced. She really did think I was an idiot.

Jeopardy tried to drag her paws, but I wrapped the leash around my hand and tugged on it so she couldn't argue. As we walked away, Heidi called, "See you in school on Monday!"

I waved and closed the gate behind me. We were just in the nick of time. I heard voices coming up one of the paths—a boy and a girl arguing loudly about which Jonas brother is cutest (I could tell the guy was just trying to make her mad) while something yapped insistently along with them.

I pulled Jeopardy along a different path, although she really, really wanted to go say hi to the new dog. I stopped farther up the hill and looked back.

The two Hispanic kids going into the dog run looked like brother and sister. The girl had dark curls and a bright pink shirt that matched her sandals. The guy was tall with spiky black hair and long green basketball shorts. His sister was holding the dog's leash, but he kept reaching for it as the puppy bounced around their feet and got them tangled up. The girl wouldn't let her brother take the leash, though; she kept pushing him away and yelling, "I'VE GOT IT! DANNY, LEAVE IT! QUIT MOVING!" The puppy was tiny and white and fuzzy and seemed delighted by their pushing and shoving.

Jeopardy made a mournful noise and I looked down at her. She looked up at me with her ears pricked, like she was hoping I'd change my mind. When I didn't head back to the dog run, her stare became a bit more accusing, like, *Well,* you *might be hopeless, but why won't you let* me *have any friends?*

"Too bad, Jeopardy," I said. I tugged her around to head out of the park. Her little paws went *trot trot trot* over the paved path. "Trust me, I'd love it if you could go to school for me on Monday. Think anyone would notice?"

Jeopardy let out a small huff, like she couldn't believe how lame I was. I kind of agreed with her. It was lame to be afraid of a new school, but I couldn't help it.

I was terrified of what would happen on Monday.

CHAPTER 3

Jeopardy didn't like it when she realized I was going somewhere on Monday. She barked and barked when Mom came in to wake me up, and then she followed me around the room with this worried, penetrating stare while I got dressed.

Downstairs, Violet was standing on a chair and banging her spoon against the table, singing one of her made-up songs about the dog in the moon and chocolate pudding. Her hair was in two messy blond pigtails, with purple berries on the elastic bands. Jeopardy went the long way around the table to avoid her, which was wise. When Violet gets excited, sometimes she grabs whatever's in front of her, even if it's a dog's tail.

Dad was at the head of the table, feeding applesauce to Violet and reading the paper at the same time. He grinned when he saw me.

"Ready for school, kiddo?" he said.

Yeah, right.

"Sure," I said. Dad was really excited about his new job, although it didn't sound any different from his old job to me—something about computers and numbers and software and stocks and yawn, I'm asleep already.

The main difference seemed to be that he wore suits to his old job, but today he had on a dark blue button-down shirt and gray pants, the same color as his eyes. He wasn't even wearing a tie. Now what were we supposed to get him for every Christmas and birthday?

I set my backpack down next to my chair while I got my cereal. Jeopardy immediately poked her nose inside, sniffing my notebooks suspiciously. I tried to nudge her away with my foot as I sat down. She stepped back, looked at me for a second, and then stuck her nose right back inside the backpack. A few minutes later, I noticed that she was trying to drag my pencil case out with her teeth. I managed to snag it back from her right before she ran off with it.

Mom hurried in, looking flustered. She thought she'd have more time to settle in before she started working as a substitute teacher at the high school, but they'd called her already with an emergency, so she had to start on Monday just like me. Which, if you ask me, was poetic justice (something else we learned about last year in fifth grade).

"What are you going to do with Jeopardy while you're at work?" I asked. Jeopardy's ears perked up and she pawed at my leg like, *I could go with you! Let's hang out! You don't look busy! Forget this school thing! Down with backpacks and pencil cases!*

"There's a day care for dogs in town," Mom said. "Your dad can drop her off while I take Violet to pre-K."

"Who's taking me?" I asked. I couldn't decide which would be worse, sharing the car with screaming Violet or staring Jeopardy.

"I'll take you, if you're ready in ten minutes," Mom said, whisking Violet off the chair. My sister yowled as Mom carried her upstairs to brush her teeth.

Dad raised his eyebrows at Jeopardy. "Whatcha think?" he said to the dog. "You want to go meet some new furry friends?"

She wagged her tail and then looked back at me like, *See,* I'm *not nervous. I'm going to make* loads *of new friends today, just you wait.*

"We'll see about that," I said to Jeopardy. "I know you. You act all excited when you meet a dog, but then when they try to be friendly, you run away again. Because you're weird, Jeopardy."

She wagged her tail harder and went "Ruff!" as if I'd made a totally genius observation.

"That's just a Sheltie thing," Dad said. "They're a little shy, but she'll warm up, especially as she spends more time with other dogs. Hey, your mom said you met someone in the park on Saturday?"

"Yeah," I said, getting up to put my bowl in the dishwasher. "She was kind of crazy, though."

"Noah!" my mom yelled from upstairs. "Five minutes!"

I'd already packed my stuff the night before, so it didn't take me long to get out the door. I really hoped I wasn't missing anything important, and that I wasn't bringing anything lame. My notebooks were all in sensible, boring colors with nothing on them, although I deliberately chose Bills colors (red, dark blue, royal blue, and white) so at least they were secretly cool. My backpack was plain red and I'd taken off the Batman and Robin buttons from Victor and Anjali. Those were kind of an inside joke, so I wasn't sure how the kids here would react to them. My polo shirt was dark blue and I was wearing khakis because I wasn't sure if jeans were allowed.

I wanted to look as normal as possible. I remembered a new kid showing up last year, in fifth grade, wearing a shirt that said I HAVE NO IDEA WHERE I AM. We all thought he was trying too hard. I didn't want to be that kid.

I also didn't want to be the kid who had to be walked into school by his mom, although I had to argue with her for a while before she agreed to let me go in by myself. I had terrible visions of Violet doing her siren impression in the halls with me standing there turning bright red.

The school was made of red brick with big windows. There was a playground not far from the parking lot with blue-and-yellow monkey bars and a slide and wood chips on the ground. We could see little kids climbing all over it as we pulled into the parking lot. Violet pressed her nose up to the window, hollering, "I WANT! I WANT!"

"Have a good day!" Mom called, rolling down the window. "Call me if you need anything!" She drove away before I could point out that I had no idea what the high school phone number was.

I spotted the main office as I came through the front door. A skinny man with bushy white eyebrows was standing outside it, glaring at the kids running past him. He was wearing a suit and looked all official, but he also looked kind of scary.

I stopped to watch him, trying to decide whether to ask him for help or try to get by him into the office. And right then someone whammed into me at full force.

As I crashed to the ground, I heard a voice yell, "RORY! Look what you DID!" It sounded like that girl from the park, Heidi.

"Oh, man, I'm sorry," said a girl's voice. She grabbed my hands and pulled me back onto my feet before I could even catch my breath. "Oh, and I don't even *know* you," she said, as if knocking over people she *did* know was totally OK.

The girl who'd crashed into me was shorter than me, with long brown hair pulled back in a ponytail. She was wearing a Red Sox T-shirt and jean shorts, although it was October and most of the other kids had on long sleeves and pants already. There were pink and purple marker scribbles all over her white Keds.

"*I* know him!" Heidi said cheerfully from behind Rory. She dusted off my backpack with a couple of vigorous *thwacks* that nearly sent me toppling over again. "We met at the dog run. He has an awesome dog!"

Rory laughed. "Heidi, all dogs are awesome to you. Are you OK, guy?"

"Yeah," I mumbled.

"You should watch where you stand," she said.

"You should watch where you run," I said. I meant it to be funny, but it came out sounding kind of obnoxious. Rory squinted at me like she couldn't tell whether I was trying to pick a fight.

"Nathan, this is Rory," Heidi barreled on as if she hadn't heard me. "Rory, this is Nathan. His dog's name is Jeopardy."

Well, that was a fantastic sign. She remembered my *dog's* name but got mine completely wrong.

"Actually—" I started to say, but the bell rang and cut me off.

"'Bye, Nathan!" Rory yelled and ran off down the hall.

"No running!" the white-haired man shouted after her. "Would you like *another* week of detention, Miss Mason?" Rory slowed down to a funny-looking fast walk and Heidi cracked up.

"Come on," she said once she'd stopped giggling.

"Mr. Peary's class is in here." She took my elbow and steered me over to a bright yellow door. We passed a big guy at his locker and he gave me a weird mean look for no apparent reason.

The desks in Mr. Peary's classroom were set up in a square with the teacher's desk along one side and students' desks along the other three. All the guys were in a clump in the middle, with girls on the two ends. I counted in my head: eight girls, six boys — plus me made seven boys.

"Hi Mr. Peary!" Heidi said brightly to the man at the front of the room. Mr. Peary looked young for a teacher, like my mom does, but he was dressed like a grown-up in a button-down green shirt and gray slacks. He had a thin brown beard and glasses that he used for reading the attendance book, then took off while he talked to the class. He set down his coffee mug and shook my hand. I noticed there was a picture of the *Mona Lisa* on the mug, but it was one of those mugs where things appear when there's hot liquid in it, so she had a cartoon mustache, beard, and beret.

"This is Nathan!" Heidi said. "Want me to pull up a desk for him?"

"That would be great, Heidi," Mr. Peary said. He glanced at a note on his desk, looking puzzled. "Did you say Nathan?"

"Actually—" I started.

SCCCRRRREEEEEEEEEEEEEEEECH!

Desk legs shrieked along the floor as Heidi dragged a desk into place at one end of the square. Mr. Peary winced and opened his mouth to stop her.

"It's Noah," I said quickly, before Mr. Peary could get distracted.

"Oh, that's what I thought," he said. "Heidi, get someone to help you, please."

I turned to reach for the desk, but a curly-haired girl was there ahead of me. She took one end and helped Heidi lift it the last few inches. Of course, now I was sitting next to a girl, several desks away from the pack of guys, who all sat together in the middle. I glanced over at them and saw a slick-looking blond guy chuckling, probably about how I'd needed two girls to move my desk for me. He elbowed the African-American kid next to him, but the second guy didn't look up from whatever he was drawing in his notebook.

The second bell rang and the last few kids dove

into their seats. My desk was next to the curly-haired girl; on the other side of her was Heidi, who nearly knocked over her chair as she jumped into it.

"All right, class," Mr. Peary said, tapping his desk with a pen. "Time to pay attention. Tara, Natasha, that includes you." Two girls on the far side of Heidi stopped whispering and gave him innocent looks. "As you may have noticed, we have a new student today. Let's all go around the room and tell him who we are—but don't worry, Noah, we know it's a lot to absorb, so we won't expect you to remember us all right away. We'll start over here." He nodded at the girl on the far side of the square from me.

"I'm Maggie," said the girl, tossing her dark curls. She had an Irish name, but she looked like she was part Native American, maybe. "You may have seen my cat, Angelina Meowly, on commercials for—"

All the guys and a couple of the girls in the class groaned loudly. The blond girl next to Maggie covered her mouth and giggled.

"What?" Maggie said, turning red. "He might have! She's on TV all the time!"

"All right, carry on," said Mr. Peary, nodding at the blond girl.

Later on, when Mr. Peary told us to take out our notebooks for math, I turned to the back of mine and tried to write down all the names I remembered. I wouldn't tell anyone this, but I actually have a pretty good memory. It helps if I write stuff down, though. Here's what I wrote about my new class, in the order they were sitting in:

Maggie: cat named Angelina Meowly???

Rebekah: blond, blue cat-shaped barrette in her hair

Eric: keeps looking at Rebekah, fiddles with a small green USB drive while he talks

Danny: Heidi's friend from the park, tall, really loud laugh

Parker: one of the only ones who looked at me when he said his name, baseball glove sticking out of his backpack

Nikos: raises his hand whenever Mr. Peary asks a question, probably the "N.S." whose essay is stapled to the Gold Star board

Brett: cheesy grin, laughed at girls moving my desk, flips his pen between his fingers like he's been practicing that for a while and hopes someone will tell him how cool it is

Jonas: quiet, hard to hear, notebooks with fish and whales and sharks on the covers, glasses

Virginia: silver rings, necklace, small dangly earrings (pierced ears), big smile, stack of horse books on her desk at free reading time, probably the "V.M." whose horse drawing is next to Nikos's essay on the Gold Star board

Natasha: one of the whispering girls, pretty, glasses, giggles at almost everything

Tara: the other whispering girl, pink beads in her hair match pink nail polish, very thin

Kristal: braces, light blue shirt that says "Big Sisters Are the Best!", split a Twix bar with Heidi at snack break

Heidi: Heidi. 'Nuff said.

Ella: supercurly brown hair, taps her fingers against her desk almost nonstop, looks like she's in another world half the time

I glanced at my list again, then crossed off the "pretty" beside Natasha's name over and over so that you couldn't read it. If anyone accidentally saw this list, I didn't want anything on there that someone could make fun of me for. I mean, she *was* pretty, but so were Rebekah and Heidi and Virginia and Tara. And maybe Ella, if she'd ever stop tapping. Plus Kristal seemed a lot nicer than Natasha; she'd leaned over to smile at me when she said her name, like Parker did.

None of the guys reminded me of Victor or Josh, though. I couldn't imagine watching football or doing crazy made-up science experiments with any of them. The only one that gave me any hope was Parker, but I could tell he was already best friends with Danny and Eric.

There was some good news. It turned out I was way ahead of the class in math—it was the same textbook, but my class in Rochester had already finished the next two chapters. The world geography lesson wasn't anything harder than capitals and mountain ranges. And everyone was reading *Holes* for English, which I'd read last year.

To be honest, I was pretty bored. I doodled in my math notebook while Mr. Peary talked about fractions. I drew footballs and buffalo and a tiny football field surrounded by a stadium full of fans.

But I was just trying to distract myself from what I knew was coming. The part of the day I dreaded most was the moment when I'd walk into the cafeteria and have to figure out where to sit.

So even though the morning seemed to go really slowly, it still felt too soon when the bell rang for lunch. I picked up my brown bag and joined the line out the door with a stomach full of butterflies.

CHAPTER 4

The cafeteria was a huge room with long, pale green tables and dark green chairs. It smelled exactly the same as our cafeteria in Rochester, kind of like ketchup and reheated pizza and sloppy joes, even though what they were actually serving was tacos. There was a separate salad bar, although only a couple of sixth graders and a bunch of teachers went over to it.

Everyone ate lunch at the same time, so the room was full of kids, most of them yelling to one another or running around the tables. It was really loud and confusing. When we got to the door, most of the kids in my class split up; some of them went straight to their tables and sat down, while others ran to the soda machine or got into the main line.

I stayed behind Danny, who'd been in front of me when we left the classroom. I figured I'd just follow whatever he did, which is how I ended up in the line for tacos.

Danny took a tray and gave me a weird look as I took one, too. "Didn't you bring your lunch?" he asked, nodding at the bag in my hand. I'd completely forgotten about it. Now I felt like an idiot.

"Um, yeah," I said. "But I really wanted some, uh . . . applesauce." I grabbed the first thing I saw. I don't even like applesauce.

"Oh, OK," Danny said. He moved along, distracted by the tacos. I took a carton of chocolate milk and followed him to the cashier. She peered at my mostly empty tray and lifted her eyebrows at me, but she took my dollar without saying anything.

"Heidi!" Danny yelled, stopping right in front of me so I nearly crashed into him. "I've been waiting to show you this all day!" He balanced his tray on one hand and started fishing through his pockets. It looked like a disaster waiting to happen.

I edged away from him and glanced around at the crowded, noisy room. Nobody even looked at me. I felt queasy.

Then somebody grabbed my arm and I jumped, knocking my milk carton to the ground.

"Oops!" Heidi said at my elbow. She knelt to pick up the carton at the same time as I did, and our heads bumped. She started laughing. "Don't tell me you're as klutzy as I am!"

"Yeah, we can only handle one Heidi in the class," Danny said to me. He waved a glossy brochure at her. "Check it out!"

Heidi took it from him and unfolded it as Danny headed for a nearby table. Parker and Eric were already there, along with a guy I didn't know and the curly-haired girl, Ella.

"Oooooh," Heidi said. I saw that there were photos of dogs on the front of the brochure. She started toward the same table and then stopped to glance back at me. "Aren't you coming?"

"Uh—sure," I said. Maybe she thought Danny had invited me to sit with them. I hoped he wouldn't mind. He did look surprised when he saw me coming, but he didn't say anything.

"I can't believe you let me call you Nathan!" Heidi said to me as I sat down in the chair next to Parker's. He grinned at me, and I felt a bit better.

"What about Nathan?" Rory said, bouncing into the chair beside Heidi. "Oh, hey, Nathan. What's up?"

"His name isn't Nathan," Heidi said. "It's *Noah*."

"Oh," Rory said, a little wrinkle appearing between her eyebrows. "That's weird. Why'd you say your name was Nathan?"

"I didn't!" I protested, but she was already getting to her feet again.

"'Bye, Rory!" Heidi called. "Rory eats lunch with her dad every day," she explained to me. "He's Coach Mason, our PE teacher; you'll meet him tomorrow. It's, like, their ritual so she can hang out with him without her stepbrother and stepsister for a little while."

"Do you play baseball?" Parker asked me. "Coach Mason's pretty great."

"Uh, no," I said. "But I guess I could."

"Only if you're good," Danny said loudly. "Because we're going to win every game this year! Yeah!"

"So's the girls' soccer team!" Heidi said.

"Noah, this is Troy," Parker said, nodding at the redheaded guy with glasses sitting a couple chairs down the table. "He's in Miss Woodhull's class." Troy gave me a halfhearted wave and went back to picking celery out of his tuna salad sandwich.

Kristal appeared with a tray of tacos, followed by Rebekah, who was one of the few kids who had a plate from the salad bar.

"What's that?" Kristal asked, nodding at Heidi's brochure as she sat down. Rebekah smiled at Eric and he blinked a lot, then smiled back at her.

"Oh, yeah," Danny said, grabbing the pamphlet. "Parker, you should see this, too. Carlos found it. It's this obedience and agility class for dogs, and it starts tonight! We totally have to go!"

Ella and Eric both leaned in to look at it. Kristal sighed and started poking her tacos with her white plastic fork.

"Aw, man, more dog talk? You guys are torturing me," said Troy. "This is totally unfair."

"Yeah," Kristal chimed in. "All you ever care about now is dog stuff." That surprised me. I couldn't think of anything to say about my dog, except maybe about how she stared at me all the time. Luckily no one seemed interested in hearing me talk. They were too busy doing all the talking themselves.

"You'll get a dog someday," Parker said to Troy.

"I won't," Kristal said, stabbing her tacos harder. "Dad is totally allergic. When we got back from your house, Parker, he sneezed for, like, half an hour because we had Merlin's fur on our jeans or something."

"Well, maybe you can come watch us train our dogs," Heidi said.

"Probably not, but *anyway*..." Danny said. He was clearly impatient to talk about the class again. "So it's only an hour long, and it meets Monday, Wednesday, and Friday nights for the next two weeks. Carlos already signed us up with Buttons. You want to go, right, Heidi?"

I realized that if I wanted to be friends with these people, I'd have to do more than memorize all their names. I'd have to remember all their *dogs'* names, too. I thought of the small white dog I'd seen with Danny on Saturday. *Buttons.* Small as a button. I could remember that.

"Mom and Dad would *love* to get Yeti trained!" Heidi said.

"But what's 'agility'?" Ella asked. "Is that like gymnastics? Or yoga?" She wrinkled her nose. "It sounds like ballet."

Heidi laughed. "No way! Agility is much more fun than ballet! I've seen it on TV—the dogs have to go through these, like, obstacle courses. They jump over hurdles and run through tunnels and climb ramps and it's superfunny. You'll like it!"

Ella looked skeptical. "That's a lot of time when I should be practicing," she said.

"But Ella," Rebekah chimed in, "if you take

Trumpet to this class, it'll tire her out. It's like taking her for a long walk or playing outside. Once you get home, she'll sleep right through your piano playing."

That made Ella look more cheerful. "OK," she said. "I'll ask Mom."

Trumpet, I said to myself. I tried picturing a trumpet with Ella's long curly hair. Hopefully that would make the name stick in my head.

"What about you, Eric?" Rebekah asked with a hopeful expression.

Eric snorted. "Are you kidding? Can you picture Meatball jumping hurdles?" Almost everyone at the table started laughing, so I smiled, too, even though I had no idea why that was so funny.

"He's amazing with that skateboard, though!" Rebekah said. "Maybe he has hidden talents. Come on, I'll sign up Noodles if you bring Meatball."

"Uh—OK," said Eric.

Meatball and Noodles. I'd have to draw a meatball on a skateboard next to Eric's name when I got back to my notebook. That should be easy to remember. I wondered what kind of dog he was.

"Yay!" Heidi cried. "This'll be so much fun!" She put her arms around Ella and Rebekah, on either side of her, and squished them into a hug.

Kristal slammed her fork down on her tray. "I'm going to the library," she said. "Not like anyone cares." She dumped everything on her tray into the garbage on her way out the door.

"Whoa," Danny said through a mouthful of taco. "What's her problem?"

"I don't know," Heidi said, looking confused. "Did I say something?"

Rebekah sighed. "Maybe she's mad because she can't come to the class."

"Or maybe she feels left out," Troy said grumpily. "Since you guys are all 'dogs dogs dogs' all the time."

There was an awkward silence. I was beginning to wish I'd sat at another table. Maybe a table with no girls at it. Girls were complicated.

"Hey, did you see the game last night?" Parker asked Troy. "With that crazy grand slam in the eighth inning?"

"I did!" Danny nearly yelled. "That was amazing!"

The four guys all started talking about baseball at once. Nobody asked me if I'd seen the game—which I hadn't, of course, because our cable wasn't hooked up yet, either.

"Hmm," Rebekah said. "*I* was watching my favorite

dance show. You guys didn't see it, did you?" she asked Heidi and Ella.

"I was practicing," Ella said.

"I was trying to find all the candy stashed in my room before Yeti finds it and eats it," Heidi said. "Oh my gosh, I had lollipops and Butterfingers and gummi bears hidden behind everything!"

Rebekah rolled her eyes, smiling. "I'll go ask Maggie if she saw it." She took her salad with her to the other table.

Heidi and Ella started talking about some new song that Ella was learning. I just sat there, eating my lunch and wishing I were back in Rochester. Kids there were a lot easier to talk to.

Then I remembered the new kid who'd shown up in fifth grade. None of us had talked to him, either. He sat by himself at lunch for the whole first month of school. I wouldn't even have noticed, but Anjali pointed it out. She said Josh and I should go say hi, but we never did. We were too busy with our own stuff. Now I couldn't even remember his name.

What if that happened to me? What if nobody *ever* talked to me? Heidi had already forgotten my name once. What if everybody else did, too?

It was too easy to imagine sitting there a month in the future, pretending to be part of a group, but really with no friends at all.

The only thing anyone said to me was at the end of lunch, as we all got up to leave. Heidi picked up the brochure again, and then smiled at me.

"Maybe you should bring Jeopardy to the class," she said. "Shelties are so smart! I bet she'd be really good at it!"

I knew better. She'd be terrible. She'd probably spend the whole class just staring at me and everyone would laugh at my weird dog. No way, no thank you.

"Nah," I said, but before I could explain why, Heidi called Rory's name and ran off across the cafeteria.

I was relieved. I figured she'd forget all about inviting me, and that would be the last I'd have to hear about this class.

I had no idea how wrong I was.

CHAPTER 5

Jeopardy and Violet were already in the car when Mom picked me up after school. Jeopardy was clipped into this goofy purple seat belt–harness thing that my dad found for her online. It's to keep her safe and stop her from bouncing around the car. She woofed at me from the backseat and tried to put her front paws up on the back of my headrest, but she couldn't reach.

"WOOF!" she said again, more grouchily.

"How was your first day?" Mom said in an overly cheerful way as I slammed the door behind me. Her hair was up in her *I'm a grown-up, take me seriously* bun.

"Fine," I said.

"MINE-SA FINE, TOO!" Violet shrieked, flinging her stuffed hippo at me. I tossed it back at her, even though I knew she'd probably just throw it at me again. If I didn't give it back to her, though, she'd start wailing, and that would be much worse.

I slouched down in my seat while we pulled out of the parking lot in a long, slow line of cars. I saw Danny getting his bike from the rack and pushing it alongside Parker and Eric and Troy as they walked off. I'd had best friends like that once upon a time. And now I had no one. No one except a crazy dog and a supersonic little sister.

"Well!" Mom said brightly. "Guess what? I signed you up for something!"

"Oh, *Mom*," I groaned. That's when I spotted a glossy, colorful piece of paper sticking out of the cup holder. Uh-oh.

"The woman at the day care was telling me about it," Mom went on. She sounded horribly excited. "Apparently they do dog training classes there, too! Doesn't that sound like fun?"

I picked up the brochure. It was exactly the one Heidi and Danny had been looking at.

"No," I said. "No way, I can't. Like, half my class is going to this."

"All the more reason!" my mom said. "It's a great way to meet people!"

Yeah, right. Try a *terrible* way to meet people. "Have you *seen* our dog, Mom? She's so embarrassing!"

"Well, I already paid for it," Mom said in her no-nonsense voice. "So if you don't go, Violet and I will have to go without you."

I wondered if Mom noticed how often she used the threat of Violet to get me to do things. If there was anything worse than suffering through this class with Jeopardy, it would be sitting at home knowing that Danny and Parker and Ella and Heidi were all hanging out with my mom and my screaming little sister, thinking I was too pathetic to take the class myself.

"RRRRRRRGH," I said, clutching my hair. But I was beaten and I knew it.

So that's how I found myself at the Bark and Ride Day Care at seven o'clock that night, standing awkwardly in the doorway with Jeopardy.

The central room was big, with a high ceiling and empty cages all the way around the walls. Paw prints in all colors, red and yellow and green and blue, were dotted along the white walls next to words like WOOF! and PAWS FOR A SNUGGLE! and other dog-related silliness. The gray floor felt bouncy under my sneakers, like in a gym or something.

Jeopardy stood next to me with her ears pricked forward. Her eyes darted around the room, from the other dogs to the row of hurdles to the tall, blond woman setting up a stretchy blue tunnel. Ella, Parker, Eric, and Danny and his little sister were already there.

I was about to go inside when big furry paws suddenly whammed against my shoulders, making me stumble forward. Jeopardy whipped around and barked frantically, which set off a whole volley of barks from the rest of the dogs.

"Oops!" Heidi cried from behind me. "Sorry!" Her hair was already falling messily out of its ponytail. She wrestled Yeti back to her side. He grinned goofily at me and Jeopardy, wagging his long black-and-white tail.

"Jeopardy, shush!" I said. "Stop it! Shhh!"

"RUFF RUFF RUFF RUFF RUFF RUFF RUFF!" she hollered, looking back and forth between me and Yeti.

"AWROOROOROOOOROOOWROOORF!" howled the beagle next to Ella.

"YAP! YAP! YAP!" the poodle puppy agreed.

"I set off a riot," Heidi said ruefully. "Typical." That surprised me, because it was really my dog who'd started all the noise. But before I could say that, Heidi said, "Hey, you came!" like she'd suddenly figured out who I was. "Awesome! Hi Jeopardy!" She crouched to pet Jeopardy, who stared at her intently while Heidi ran her fingers through the Sheltie's long honey-and-white fur. After a moment, Jeopardy backed away and leaned against my leg.

"All right, let's get started!" the woman called. Heidi and I hurried into the big room. As we took our places, Rebekah came running in behind us, carrying a tiny bundle of brown-and-white fluff.

The instructor's name was Alicia, and her dog's name was Parsnip. He was about Jeopardy's size, with long black fur and a sweet terrier face. Alicia said he was a mutt—part Jack Russell, part Scottie, part papillon, and she had no idea what else. Parsnip sat politely at Alicia's side the whole time she talked. The poodle puppy was desperately trying to get over to him to say hi, but he just wagged his tail a little bit at her and stayed right where he was, even though he didn't have a leash on or anything.

Buttons, I reminded myself, watching the poodle. That's what Danny had said at lunch. His little sister had sparkly pink heart barrettes in her curly dark hair and pink glitter on her shoes. There was an older boy with them, too. Luckily I didn't have to try to remember his name, because the little sister kept yelling: "CARLOS, GIVE ME THE LEASH! I'M DOING IT FINE! CARLOS, STOP IT!" So I guessed that was Carlos. And when he yelled back, "ROSIE, JUST LISTEN TO ME!", that was a pretty good clue that her name was Rosie.

We all stood in a semicircle around Alicia, holding on to our dogs' leashes while she talked. Some of the dogs didn't seem to mind, like Heidi's dog, who just smiled and panted and looked around as if he was perfectly happy no matter what happened. Others, like Jeopardy and Buttons, kept leaning around trying to say hi to everyone else.

I tried to remember the other dogs' names. I thought of my mental picture of the trumpet with curly hair—so the tricolor beagle next to Ella must be Trumpet. She had brown ears, a white chest and paws, and black fur on her back. She kept looking up at Ella with huge, adoring brown eyes. I glanced down at Jeopardy. She was watching me, too, but her little black eyes didn't look adoring to me. They looked kind of impatient, like even my standing around was too slow for her.

Rebekah put her small fluffy dog on the floor next to Eric's bulldog. Noodles and Meatball—that name was easy to remember now that I saw what a funny roly-poly pudge-dog he was. The bulldog immediately got low to the ground and rolled onto his back in front of Noodles, wriggling happily and snorting like a buzz saw.

"We're going to start with the basics," Alicia said, clapping her hands. Alicia's blond hair was pulled back in a braid. She had a serious face and a sharp nose, and she looked like she could easily run to Canada and back in like an hour if she wanted to. I felt like *I* would probably sit if she told me to.

"How many of your dogs know how to sit?" she asked.

Buttons stopped straining at the end of her leash and promptly sat down. Jeopardy was already sitting, and so was Noodles, leaning forward to sniff Meatball's fat white belly. None of the other dogs moved, except for Yeti's tail, which was swishing back and forth like he was trying to start a hurricane. There was a shiny golden retriever next to Parker who kept looking over at Yeti like he desperately wanted to go make friends.

"Trumpet sits sometimes," Ella said, giving her beagle a dubious look. "If the treats are worth it."

"Having great treats is the best way to get their attention," Alicia said. She came around and gave us each a little treat bag to hook on to our belts. Mine was blue and so was Heidi's. The treats were small and square and smelled like bacon. Jeopardy propped her front paws on my leg and leaned up to poke the bag with her nose.

"Not until you sit," I said. To my surprise, she dropped back down and sat. I knew my dad had been working on teaching her that, but I didn't know she'd really learned it. I fished out a treat and gave it to her.

"SNOOOORRRRRRG," said Meatball, rolling up onto his paws and staring at Jeopardy while she chomped down her treat. She gave him a satisfied look like, *Well, it's just because I'm a genius and you're not, that's all.*

Alicia showed us the hand signal we were supposed to use to get the dogs to sit—holding one hand out flat, palm up, while we said "Sit!" in a firm voice.

Only Buttons and Jeopardy did it every time. Yeti kept getting distracted by the other dogs. He'd start to sit, and then hear Parker saying "Sit!" behind him. So then he'd whirl around to find out who else was sitting and whether their treats were any better than his.

Trumpet would sniff the treat, then look at Ella like she was checking to make sure Ella really, *really* wanted her to sit. Then after Ella said "Sit!" a few more times, Trumpet sighed and slowly lowered her butt to the floor.

"Merlin, sit!" Parker said. Merlin was the golden retriever. I didn't know how I'd remember that name, but he was a really handsome dog. His pink tongue hung out as he grinned at Parker. At first he kept wagging his tail and smiling instead of sitting, but he picked it up eventually.

Meatball was the funniest, though. Once Eric finally got him to sit, Meatball refused to stand back up again. He gazed around the room, breathing snortily through his nose. It was really loud. Eric kept waving the treat in front of his nose to make him stand, but Meatball just crossed his eyes at it and tried to take it without getting up.

This made Rebekah laugh too much to concentrate on Noodles, who kept circling around Rebekah's feet and getting the leash all tangled up while she yipped at the other dogs. Her soft brown-and-white fur fluffed out as she bounced around. I wondered what kind of dog she was—I guessed a mix of some kind, although I didn't know much about really small dogs.

It was noisy and chaotic with all the dogs getting excited at once. But I was actually relieved. Jeopardy was being much better than I expected, especially compared to the other dogs. Maybe she was pretty smart after all.

I should have known it wouldn't last.

CHAPTER 6

The trouble started with the hurdles.

After we'd all practiced "sit" for a while, Alicia brought us over to a part of the room where there were three hurdles set up in a row. They looked like big white capital H's, except the middle bar was set low to the ground—only about a hand's width from the floor for the first hurdle, and a little higher on each of the others. The white tubes were decorated with bright green stripes. There was a lot of space between each hurdle, enough for two dogs Yeti's size to stand end to end.

"This should be fun for both you and your dog," Alicia said. "The command you're going to use is 'over.' Watch." She walked toward the first hurdle with Parsnip trotting at her heels. Facing the hurdle, Alicia swung her hand toward it and said, "Over!" She used the hand on the same side that Parsnip was on. Parsnip ran right up to the hurdle and jumped over it, then sat down and waited for his treat.

"So that's what you're working toward," Alicia said. "But we'll start with—"

She didn't get to finish her sentence, because Rosie was already running at the hurdle with Buttons bouncing along at her heels. "Buttons, OVER!" Rosie yelled, flapping both hands at the hurdle like she was conducting an orchestra.

To everyone's surprise, Buttons leaped right over the bar, then jumped over it in the other direction to get back to Rosie. The puppy capered around Rosie's knees, wagging her tail frantically like she was saying, *Did I do it right? Was that it? Was I amazing? I was, wasn't I?*

"Good dog! Good dog!" Rosie cried, dropping about twenty treats on Buttons' head as she clipped the puppy's leash back on. Buttons gobbled up all the ones that fell on the floor and then turned around and around, looking confused. She could smell another treat somewhere, but she couldn't figure out that it was stuck in the fluffy fur on top of her head.

"That *was* very good," Alicia said, rescuing the treat and giving it to Buttons. "She's a natural. But let's all take turns, OK?" She turned to the rest of us. "It's more likely that you'll have to lure your dog over the hurdle the first time, using a treat. You can put it in front of their nose, or throw it over so they'll follow it. Heidi, give it a try."

Heidi led Yeti up to the hurdle and took off his leash. "Yeti, over!" she said, sending her hand forward exactly like Alicia had. It looked like she was pushing something through the air, or bowling an invisible bowling ball.

Yeti stopped in his tracks and started sniffing Heidi's hand. Heidi giggled. "OK, silly," she said. She pulled a treat out of the little bag. "Here, follow this." She put the treat in front of Yeti's nose and made him follow it through the hurdle. Yeti's dark eyes were focused on the treat the whole time. He was so intent on watching it that he didn't look down at the bar. His enormous white paws bumped right into it, knocking the pole onto the floor. Yeti didn't even seem to notice.

"Goofy!" Heidi said. "Knocking things over is *my* job!" But she ruffled the fur on his head and gave him the treat anyway. He wagged his tail happily.

"That's OK, it's a good start," Alicia said. "We'll work on it."

Alicia set the pole back into place and beckoned Parker forward. Merlin sniffed the treat that Parker held in front of his nose. Then when Parker tossed the treat over the hurdle, Merlin jumped right after it.

"Perfect," Alicia said, smiling at Merlin. "Ella?"

It took a couple of treats, but Trumpet finally stepped gingerly over the hurdle. She kept giving Ella this furrowed-brow expression like, *WHY are you making me do this? What is the ultimate goal, exactly?*

Meanwhile, Jeopardy was leaning forward at the end of her leash, staring at the dogs as they went over the hurdle one at a time. I had to really dig my feet in to hold her in place. Even when I waved a treat at her and told her to sit, she only glanced back at me, rolled her eyes at the treat, and went back to staring at the hurdle.

Eric went next, which was really funny. As soon as he pulled out a treat, Meatball sat down, right in front of the hurdle. He looked up at Eric with an expression that said, *This is what you wanted, right? I mean, you've been telling me to sit for the last ten minutes. Look how good I am at it now! I could sit here all day!*

"Come on, Meatball!" Eric said. "Over!" He waved his hand toward the hurdle.

"Make sure you use your right hand," Alicia said, "since he's on your right side at the moment. Lean into it like you're propelling him forward. Great agility dogs will read your movements carefully and respond to little signals."

"SNOOOOOOOOOOOORRRRRRRRRRRRRRRRRRGH," Meatball offered. His enormous tongue flapped up and down as he panted.

"I think he just said 'Yeah, Eric! If you were using the right hand I'd know exactly what to do!'" Danny said. He and Parker and Heidi all started laughing.

"Ha ha ha," Eric said. He looked flustered. He ran his hands through his straight black hair, which made it stick up at the top. He glanced at Rebekah, who had picked up Noodles and was cuddling her while she waited for her turn.

"Come *on*, Meatball," Eric said. He leaned down and tugged on Meatball's collar, but the bulldog refused to stand up. Eric stuck the treat in front of his nose. Meatball studied it for a long moment, then tried to grab it out of Eric's hand. But Eric moved it quickly forward, holding it out over the hurdle.

Meatball sighed, like this was really quite inconvenient for him. He lowered his head and sniffed at the bar of the hurdle. Then he swung his big head around to stare longingly at Noodles.

"Meatball!" Eric said firmly. "Over!" He poked the treat in front of Meatball's nose again and then tossed it right over the bar like Parker had.

Meatball watched the treat hit the floor on the other side. Slowly, very slowly, he lumbered to his feet. He put one front paw over the hurdle bar, then the other front paw. With half of him on one side of the hurdle and half of him on the other, he was able to reach down and snarf up the treat.

CHOMP SNORT CHOMPFLE SNORFT, he rumbled, smacking his lips as he ate it. He looked immensely pleased with himself.

Eric threw up his hands. "Meatball!" he cried.

"That's OK!" Alicia said quickly. "That's a very good start! Bulldogs are . . . let's just say, they're not always too fond of agility. Quick, run around to that side and lure him all the way over with another treat."

Eric did as she said, and Meatball finally stepped all the way over the bar. He wrinkled his forehead while Eric clipped the leash back on, like he was thinking, *That was an awful lot of fuss about nothing. What just happened?*

Rebekah had trouble with Noodles, too. The brown-and-white puppy kept running around the hurdle to grab the treat instead of jumping over it. She poked the bar with her nose and then scampered in a circle around the whole thing.

"Noodles, come back!" Rebekah said, laughing. She held the treat on the closer side and Noodles ran back around to her. "No, jump *over*, silly!"

Alicia showed Rebekah the hand movement again. They both got down on the floor and kept the treat close to Noodles, encouraging her with lots of happy noises when she got close to the bar. Finally, with a little yip, Noodles put her front paws right on the bar and boosted herself over.

"Yay!" Rebekah cried. "What a good girl! Good girl, Noodles! Such a good puppy!"

Noodles ran around the hurdle and jumped into Rebekah's lap. Her long fluffy tail was going nuts and she kept jumping up to lick Rebekah's face. She climbed onto Rebekah's shoulder and peered over it at Meatball like, *Did you see me? I was awesome!*

At last it was my turn. I was pretty nervous, because Jeopardy was quietly freaking out. She couldn't take her eyes off the hurdle. I heard her go "ooorf! rroorrf!" in this tiny, whimpering kind of way while she watched the other dogs. Her white front paws went up and down, up and down on the rubber floor beside me, like she was practicing dance steps in her head or getting ready to start a race. By the time Alicia called us, Jeopardy was up on her back paws and straining at the end of her leash. As I stepped forward, she went: "ARF! ARF!" like she was shouting, *FINALLY! FINALLY!*

I stopped in front of the hurdle. Jeopardy's whole furry body was quivering with excitement. I leaned down to unclip her leash.

"OK, Jeopardy —" I started, but before I could say "over!" — actually, before I even finished her name — Jeopardy was gone. She leaped over that first hurdle and kept going. *Zip!* She went over the second hurdle. *Swish!* She flew over the third hurdle. "ARF ARF ARF ARF ARF!" she barked as she jumped, and then she kept barking at the top of her lungs as she bolted around the room.

"ARF ARF ARF ARF ARF ARF ARF ARF ARF!" She galloped in a huge circle around all of us, barking frantically.

"Jeopardy!" I yelled. "Get over here!"

"ARF ARF ARF ARF ARF!" she answered, flying like the wind from one wall to another. She looked both blissful and smugly triumphant, like she'd managed to fool me and escape and now she was having the time of her life.

I wanted to sink into the floor. Rosie put her hands on her hips like she'd never seen anything so disorderly in her life. She looked even more disapproving than Alicia.

"Jeopardy, come!" Alicia said firmly.

"ARF ARF ARF!" Jeopardy barked, darting forward and then dashing out of reach again as Alicia reached for her. Eric and Rebekah had their hands over their ears. Heidi and Ella were laughing hysterically.

"Jeopardy!" I shouted. "Stop! Stay!" I ran at her, but she ducked away from me, too. I threw myself forward to grab her collar and missed. My chin hit the bouncy floor with a painful *thwack*.

"Oh my gosh!" Heidi cried, clapping her hands to her mouth. "Noah, are you OK?"

"Yeah," I said, although my jaw hurt like crazy. Jeopardy stopped and stared at me from a few feet away.

"Aw, see, she feels bad," Heidi said, clasping her hands together.

I wasn't so sure about that. Her face was more like, *Why did you stop playing? What's wrong with you? Why are you so lame?*

"Come here!" I said.

"ARF!" Jeopardy answered and ran off with her tail wagging.

"Here," Parker said, handing Merlin's leash to Danny. "Let's corner her." He chased Jeopardy around the shiny blue tunnel. She raced toward the wall and we both ran at her from either side. Even so, she nearly slipped through our hands again, but I threw my arms over her back and tackled her to the floor.

Immediately she relaxed. As I lay on top of her, gasping for air, she craned her head back and licked my ear. "Ruff," she said calmly, like, *So that was fun. Now what?*

"Thanks," I said to Parker. He took the leash out of my hand and snapped it onto Jeopardy's collar.

"No problem," he said. He shook his brown hair out of his eyes and patted Jeopardy's head. "That's totally happened to me with Merlin."

I glanced over at the perfect golden retriever as I got to my feet. Merlin was sitting next to Danny with his head tilted curiously, as if he was wondering whether it would be safe to join our game or if Jeopardy was too insane.

"Really?" I said. It was hard to imagine having to chase Merlin down.

Parker rolled his eyes. "You have no idea," he said.

I dragged Jeopardy back to our spot. Alicia was waiting with her eyebrows raised.

"I'm sorry," I said.

"Don't be," she said. "I think it's a good sign that she's excited about the equipment. She's a very smart little dog. But we might have to leave her leash on for a while, at least at first, so we don't have to chase her every time."

"Aww," Danny said. "But it's so funny to watch!" He imitated Jeopardy's face as she ran away from us.

Everyone laughed. Ella leaned over to whisper something to Heidi. I was sure they were talking about what a terrible dog owner I was. It didn't help me at all that Jeopardy was a "very smart little dog"; as far as I could tell, that just made me look even dumber next to her. I'd much prefer an ordinary-smart dog like Merlin or Yeti.

My face felt like it was burning up. Nobody else had to leave their dog's leash on. Nobody else had a crazy dog like mine. Nobody else's dog took up all the class time by acting like a lunatic.

Why was *my* dog always the worst behaved?

CHAPTER 7

How was it?" Mom asked as I let Jeopardy into the backseat of the car. My hands were shaking as I clipped the dog's seat belt around her. She lifted one paw to help me fit the harness on. I leaned around her to snap the belt into place and she nosed at my face with her soft muzzle. But if she was asking forgiveness, it was way too late for that.

"Awful," I said. I got in the front seat and slammed the door behind me. "Jeopardy's a pain. That was the longest hour of my life."

Mom looked worried. "What happened?" she asked. "I always thought she was such a smart little dog."

"Yeah, that's exactly the problem," I said. "She's so smart she can do the course by herself! She doesn't even need me. I'm just here to look like an idiot and amuse her."

"Surely it wasn't that bad," said Mom.

"I don't want to talk about it." I slouched in the seat and crossed my arms. Through the front window I could see Heidi trying to squish Yeti into the backseat of her parents' car. His big head poked out one window while the tip of his tail peeked out the opposite side. Heidi was laughing, as usual. I wished I thought my dog was funny. I wished my dog *was* funny, instead of just obnoxious.

"What happened to your chin?" Mom asked.

Uh-oh. I flipped the visor down to look at myself in the mirror. There was a gross red scrape along the bottom of my chin. Seeing it made it hurt even more.

"I *really* don't want to talk about it," I said.

At home I went straight up to my room, but it didn't make me feel any better, because my stuff was still scattered everywhere. It was a mess. That was how the inside of my head felt, too. I didn't know what to do—unpack some more or clean up what I'd already unpacked or finish my homework, which was all really easy stuff I'd already done. What I *wanted* to do was throw something at the wall.

Well, OK. What I really wanted to do was go back to Rochester and play video games with Victor while we ate all of Josh's mom's brownies. I just wanted to be a guy who had friends again. Someone that everyone already knew, so if something embarrassing or weird happened, it didn't matter, because your friends knew what you were really like.

Just thinking about trying to talk to people at lunch the next day made me tired. I sat down on the bed and kicked aside a pile of white socks on the floor. I remembered Rory's face when she thought I'd lied about my name for no reason. She'd barely spoken to me twice, but she was convinced I was a weirdo. And I hadn't even done anything.

Scratch scratch scratch.

I knew that sound. Jeopardy was at the door, asking to come in. As if I'd ever be speaking to her again.

I lay down on the bed and ignored her.

Scratch scratch scratch.

What was I going to do on Wednesday? Quit? Let Mom take Jeopardy to the class without me? I was pretty sure the others would think that was pretty pathetic. They'd be like, *I guess Noah is intimidated by how smart his dog is. Well, that's fine; we didn't want him here anyway!*

Knock knock.

I nearly ignored the knock on the door, too, until

I remembered that Jeopardy couldn't exactly do that. "Yeah?" I called.

Dad opened the door and stuck his head inside. "Hey, champ," he said. Jeopardy immediately shoved her way between his legs and the door and came charging across the room toward me. She put her front paws up on the bed next to my head and stared down at me, panting and smiling a little in her weird way. I kept my eyes on the ceiling and refused to look at her.

"Guess what?" Dad said. "There's a football game on. Want to watch it with me?"

"Really?" I said. I sat up, and Jeopardy wagged her tail. "We have TV now? What about the Internet?"

"All set up," Dad said proudly, like he was expecting some kind of Nobel Prize for finally figuring that out. "Come on downstairs. I got an apple pie for dessert."

OK, now I knew he was feeling guilty. Apple pie is my favorite.

I got my laptop and followed him down to the living room. There's a little sunroom off to the side of the living room, which Mom and Dad filled with Violet's toys so it could be her playroom. She was in there on a big plastic fire truck that used to be mine, rolling around and going "WEEEEEEE-OOOOOOOOOOO-WEEEEEEEEEEE-OOO-OOOOOO-WEEEEEEE-OOOOOOOOOO" at the top of her lungs.

"That's not going to be distracting at all," I muttered. Dad had the TV paused in the middle of a football game. It wasn't the Bills, but at least it was something on the TV screen besides Violet's *Dora the Explorer* and *Backyardigans* DVDs that she'd been watching all weekend. I bet those shows would be a lot less annoying if Violet didn't yell along with the dialogue and then sing the theme song for the rest of the day.

Dad showed me how to set up the wireless access on my laptop, and then he went off to get apple pie for us while I *finally* checked my e-mail. None of my friends were signed into IM, but they'd all written to me saying they missed me and school wasn't the same without me and that I'd better write every day and stuff like that.

Anjali had sent me a photo of her two chinchillas nibbling on a sign that said, WE MISS YOU, NOAH! Their names are Rama and Sita, after this couple in a famous Indian legend called the Ramayana, which Anjali loves. Last Halloween she even made them tiny sparkly outfits like the mythological Rama and Sita might wear, but the chinchillas tried to eat the sequins, so she had to take them off again.

The whole time I was checking my e-mail, Jeopardy stood next to my knees and stared at me. At one point, Violet went "WEEEEEEEYAAAAA-OOOOO!" extra loudly and Jeopardy jumped, gave the sunroom a suspicious look, then went back to staring at me. Well, if she wanted me to invite her up on the couch, it wasn't going to happen.

It did get a little annoying, though. "Go away," I said to her. I was trying to e-mail Josh about how awful the dog class had been.

Jeopardy sidled a bit closer so her fur was brushing against my khakis.

"Stop it," I said. "Go bug somebody else."

She waited for another minute while I ignored her. Finally she jumped up on the couch, turned around three times, and settled down with a sigh, resting her chin on the curve of my elbow. I looked down at her and she looked up at me with serious black eyes.

"I'm not forgiving you," I said. My chin was still in pain, and it would probably look really stupid tomorrow.

But I let her leave her head on my elbow. It was

better than having her stare at me. When Dad came back with apple pie and chocolate chip ice cream, I put away my laptop and we watched the rest of the game together. Jeopardy fell asleep curled up next to me. Her breath went *snrrzzz snnrrrzzz* through her nose.

"That dog thinks you're the bomb," Dad said during a commercial break.

I didn't want to make him feel better, but I couldn't help it. I started laughing. "Dad, nobody says that anymore."

"Really?" he asked, scraping pie from the bottom of his bowl. "I'm not that old, am I?"

"Also, you're wrong," I added. "Jeopardy's whole purpose in life is to make me miserable." The dog's ears twitched a little in her sleep when I said her name.

"EEEEEEEEEEEEEEYAAAAAAAAAAA-AAAAAOOOOOOOOOOOO!" Violet shrieked, running through the room waving a stuffed hippo over her head. She has kind of a thing about hippos, too. And if they're purple, it's like the greatest thing she's ever seen.

"I thought making you miserable was Violet's job," Dad said with a grin. I heard Mom scoop up my sister and carry her howling up the stairs to bed.

"Yeah," I said. "They're in cahoots."

Now Dad started laughing and couldn't stop. "Cahoots! I can't say 'the bomb' but you can say 'cahoots'? Are you kidding me?"

"I'm the eleven-year-old," I pointed out. "I automatically know what's cool and you don't."

"Ah, of course," he said. "Silly me." He kept chuckling and mumbling "cahoots" for the rest of the game. It was a lot quieter after Violet went to bed. It's OK to be quiet with Dad; he doesn't need to ask me a million questions about my day like Mom does. I realized at one point that I'd forgotten to be upset for at least half an hour. Everything felt like it did back in Rochester—same couch, same TV, same football with my dad, same furry dog curled up next to us, although normally she did more staring and less sleeping, so this was actually a bit of an improvement.

If only I didn't have to go to school again, things might not have seemed so bad.

CHAPTER 8

But I did have to go to school, and Tuesday was even worse than Monday.

First I couldn't remember which door was Mr. Peary's, so I had to kind of wander around the hall pretending I knew where I was until I saw Jonas and followed him to the classroom. All the other sixth graders were at their bright blue and green lockers, talking and joking.

I hadn't even tried finding my locker yet, although Mr. Peary had taken me to the office after school the day before to get me a locker number and combination. We didn't have lockers in my old elementary school—even here they were just for the fifth and sixth graders—so I was used to carrying all my books around. What if I forgot something I needed because I left it in my locker? It seemed safer to keep it all with me.

Jonas and I were the first people in the classroom.

Not even Mr. Peary was there yet. Jonas sat down at his desk and pulled out a book about whales. He didn't say anything to me. He looked like a taller, skinnier version of Josh, if Josh ever wore glasses, which is maybe why I was stupid enough to try to talk to him.

"Hey, uh," I said, brilliantly. Jonas looked up, and then around the room like he was trying to figure out who I was talking to.

"Uh, you like fish?" I asked. Oh, that was *genius*, Noah.

Jonas blinked. I pointed at the book he was reading.

"Whales aren't fish," he said, and went back to reading.

"I know!" I said. "I know that!" I really did. They're mammals. Everyone knew that. "I mean, just 'cause of your notebooks and . . . stuff . . . "

He gave me a look like I was some kind of stalker. But dude, it wasn't hard to figure out. He had a wriggly plastic purple squid hanging from a loop on his dark blue backpack. Whenever he raised his hand during science, he usually had a question about the ocean. His free reading book yesterday had a sea turtle on the cover. Maybe I noticed stuff, but it didn't take Sherlock Holmes to guess that Jonas was interested in ocean life.

Luckily I didn't have to find out what he'd say next, because the classroom door flew open and Rory burst in. Her cheeks were pink from running and her long brown hair had fallen out of its ponytail.

"Where's Heidi?" she demanded, shoving her hair out of her face. It was longer than I'd realized, all the way down to her waist and really straight.

Jonas and I stared at her blankly. As if either of us would know?

Rory snorted. "You guys are a big help," she said. As she turned back to the door she stopped, backed up, and squinted at my face.

"Yikes!" she said. "What happened to you?"

I ducked my head and touched my chin, feeling like Frankenstein's monster. "Nothing," I muttered. "My stupid dog." Or not-stupid-enough dog, I guess would be more accurate.

"Wicked. I've got one on my elbow just like that," Rory said, pushing up the sleeve of her red T-shirt so I could see the huge scrape that went up her arm. "And over here." She held out her other hand, where the skin on her palm was shiny and pink like it had just healed. "And let's not even talk about my knees."

She glanced down at the scars and scabs on her knees and shins. I hadn't noticed them before. "This is from when I broke my leg last summer." She pointed at a shiny scar on her left leg. "I tried to skateboard off a flight of steps." She wrinkled her nose at the surprised face I made. "I had to! Danny dared me to!"

"I broke my arm two summers ago," I said, showing her the fading scar. "Climbing a tree. Well, technically, falling out of a tree."

"I was seven when I broke *my* arm," Rory said proudly. "Jumped off the roof with an umbrella."

"Nobody really does that!" I said, trying not to laugh.

"They do if their best friend has watched *Mary Poppins* too many times!" Rory said. She glanced over at Heidi's desk and then at her watch. "Really it was her idea. And her umbrella, by the way. It was black and white with floppy ears so it looked like a dog's face. I totally smashed it when I landed."

"Don't tell my little sister you did that," I said. "You'll give her ideas."

"I have a little sister, too," Rory said, smiling. "Well, stepsister. She's the one who did this to my Keds." She waved one foot to show off the highlighter scribbles.

"How old—" I started to ask, but a voice interrupted me.

"Hey Rory," it said. It was the tall blond guy I didn't like—Brett, if I remembered right. He strolled around Rory and rested his butt on Ella's desk. "How *is* your sister? Cameron, right? Did she ever find her lunch money?"

"No!" Rory said, looking mad, but not at Brett. Which was too bad. I didn't want to find out she was friends with this guy. "She sulked about it all weekend."

Brett shook his hair back and smiled in a greasy way. He hadn't even looked at me once. His butt slid over a few inches so it was nearly on my desk, slowly putting him between me and Rory.

"You know," he said in a low voice, "I bet Avery's been stealing other things, too." I wondered who Avery was. There was a girl named Avery in my class back in Rochester, but I didn't think I'd met any Averys here yet.

Rory shrugged. "Well, I'll find out eventually. Whatever happened to it, it was really annoying. Cameron acted like a total brat to poor little Cormac all weekend." She was a lot shorter than Brett, so she had to look up at him to talk to him. A lock of her hair drifted over her shoulder, and she picked it up and started twisting it around her finger.

For some reason, it made me kind of mad, the way she was doing that and looking up at him. I wanted her to be like, "OK, go away, Brett, Noah and I were talking."

"Uh," Brett said, scratching his head. "Cormac . . ."

"My stepbrother," Rory said. She dropped her hair and stepped back, looking at her watch again. "Uh-oh! I better go. Miss Woodhull yells at me *all the time* for being late." She hurried to the door. "'Bye, Nathan!" she called as she went through it.

Oh, GREAT. I'd finally had a normal conversation with someone, and she didn't even know what my name was. What was wrong with the girls at this school?

Brett smirked at me and strolled over to his seat next to Jonas.

"Oops," Rory said, sticking her head back in. "I mean Noah. Right? Noah?"

"Uh, yeah," I stammered. "That's right."

"Next time you move, don't confuse people like that!" she said, and vanished out the door again.

Next time I moved? Unless it was back to Rochester, I was never moving again. And if I did, I'd get some kind of radar to avoid meeting people like Heidi, who remembered your dog's name better than your own.

A minute later, I felt bad for having that thought when Heidi bounced through the door and waved at me with a big smile.

"Wasn't class awesome last night?" she said. "I can't wait for Wednesday!"

Oh, I could wait for Wednesday. If it were up to me, I'd have been perfectly happy if Wednesday never came.

CHAPTER 9

School was just as boring on Tuesday as it was on Monday, maybe even worse. I nearly fell asleep while Mr. Peary talked about moving from the Egyptians to the Greeks during social studies. I did a whole project on Greek myths about Apollo (the sun god) back in Rochester. In fifth grade my biography project was on Alexander the Great, who came from Macedonia and conquered Greece plus, like, half the known world, which made him pretty cool if you asked me. I still remembered the name of his horse (Bucephalus) and everything.

I doodled all over my notebook again, and when that got boring, I built a football field on my desk using pens and erasers and a couple of paperback books for the bleachers. I was pretty excited when it was time for PE because I could finally *do* something.

In Rochester we'd had PE three times a week, but here it was only on Tuesdays and Thursdays, in the middle of the morning. I hoped we'd get to do something with a lot of running, like maybe football or soccer. I didn't always kick the ball in the right direction, but I was the fastest runner in my grade at my old school.

Coach Mason shook my hand when Mr. Peary introduced me, and I remembered he was Rory's dad. I could kind of see that they had the same brown eyes and the same way of standing with their hands on their hips, leaning forward a little when they were watching something.

We had PE outside with the other two sixth grade classes, so everyone was all mixed together and there were a lot more people I didn't know. I saw Troy from our lunch table and the big guy who'd glared at me on the first day. He was kind of glaring at everyone, though, so I guessed maybe it wasn't personal. Well, I *hoped* it wasn't personal. He was pretty darn big.

Coach Mason started by having us do stretches and warm-ups, and then he told us to run around the track for ten minutes. It was kind of chilly outside, but still not as cold as it would be in Rochester in

October, and once I started running I warmed up pretty quick.

Most of the other kids ran in small clumps, talking to each other while they ran. Tara and Natasha were barely jogging; mostly they pointed at people and laughed and tossed their hair. Jonas was also going pretty slowly, talking nonstop to a quiet Indian guy, which surprised me because Jonas didn't seem to talk much to anyone in our class, except maybe Nikos sometimes.

Parker, Danny, Eric, and Troy ran together, of course, laughing and shoving one another until Coach Mason yelled at them to cut it out. I started out right behind them, but when I saw a break to their right, I sped up and ran past them. For a moment I was afraid Danny would yell some joke at me, but he didn't even stop talking to notice me going by.

The wind blew in my face and my sneakers went *thud thud thud* on the track in a perfect smooth rhythm. I felt like I could run forever. I ran past Nikos and an Asian guy I didn't know; past a pair of twin girls fighting about something; past the big, mean-looking guy, who was running slowly by himself and sweating already; past a girl with dark, curly hair who had to keep stopping to pick up her giant earrings as they fell out over and over again; past Virginia and Maggie and a girl who looked like Sasha Obama, whose silver bracelets jangled as she ran. Nobody said anything to me as I ran by them.

Then I saw Brett up ahead of me, and I slowed down. He was running with a couple of guys from Mr. Guare's class, and I had a feeling he wouldn't let me pass them without making some snide comment.

"Jeez, finally!" Rory's voice said behind me. I glanced around as Heidi and Rory panted up next to me. "Man, you're fast!" Rory said. "We've been trying to catch up to you for ages!"

"We should have just slowed down," Heidi said with a laugh. "Then he could have caught up to us instead!"

"Uh . . . sorry," I said. I slowed down a bit more so we could all run side by side. I couldn't figure out why they'd been trying to catch up to me. And was it weird to run with girls? I sneaked a glance around. None of the other guys were running with a girl.

"Does it hurt?" Heidi asked, peering at my chin. "Ow. It looks like it hurts."

"Not much," I said with a shrug, although it stung a little when the wind hit it.

"You should have seen the scrape Heidi had on

her nose in fourth grade!" Rory said. "It was hilarious! She looked like one of those modern paintings where everything is in the wrong place."

"Like Picasso?" I asked.

"Who?" she said. "I mean, sure. What'd you do, again, Heidi? Fall out of bed?"

"Probably. I fall down a lot," Heidi said ruefully.

"Me too," Rory agreed.

"Nuh-uh!" Heidi said. "You don't fall off things! You jump off them, or bike off them, or roller-skate off them, and *then* you fall! It's not the same as being clumsy when you're doing it on purpose!"

Rory laughed, and then Coach Mason blew the whistle, so we all ran back over to him. To my surprise, he'd brought out a bunch of Frisbees. We'd never played Frisbee at my old school. Coach Mason divided us into teams, which was awesome for me because that way I didn't have to wait to be picked last, as I'm sure I would have been. Tara and Natasha complained a lot when he split them up, but considering they spent the whole game standing with each other anyway and ducking whenever the Frisbee came their way, it didn't really make much difference.

Running around with the Frisbee was the last good part of the day. After that it was time for lunch, and it took me a whole ten minutes to work up the courage to go sit at Danny's table again. Parker nodded at me, but everyone was listening to Troy talking about some mystery-crime show, so most of them didn't even say hi. Kristal wasn't there, but nobody said anything about that. Nobody said anything to me at all. I ate my lunch feeling stupid and out of place.

Then we had a long, super-boring afternoon. At the end of the day I tried to find my locker, but Brett was leaning on it and talking to the girl with the silver bracelets, so I gave up. I headed out to the parking lot with all my books. Nobody said good-bye. Everyone had someone else to talk to.

I finally found my mom's car and climbed in. Violet shrieked hello from the backseat and Jeopardy went "Ruff! Ruff! Ruff!" at me and then out the window. "Ruff! Ruff! Ruff!" A bunch of kids turned to stare at her.

"Shush!" I said. She wagged her tail and smiled at me. She completely couldn't tell when I was mad at her. So much for that giant brain of hers.

"Make any new friends today?" Mom asked hopefully.

I rolled my eyes at her. That seemed like enough of an answer. But as we drove home I thought about Rory. Maybe she could kind of be a friend. She'd been amazing with the Frisbee. I wouldn't mind playing Frisbee with her sometime . . . if she could just remember my name.

I finished my homework in no time and then tried to clean up my room some more. Jeopardy followed me around the house all night, watching everything I did. If I picked something up and then put it down, she'd immediately grab it in her mouth and back away like she was hoping I would chase her for it.

She circled around my legs while I went up and down the stairs and nearly tripped me at least five times. She jumped up on a chair by my window and barked at everything that went by on the street — cars, people, cats, invisible specks of dust (apparently). She pawed at my knee whenever I sat down. She kept hiding things under my bed. She couldn't stay still for two seconds.

Dad came in while I was sitting on the floor, unpacking books onto my shelf. Jeopardy was pacing back and forth between me and the door, sniffing everything thoroughly and then sniffing it again. She barked and ran over to my dad, then ran back to me, then ran back to him.

"Jeopardy, CHILL!" I shouted. She ran back to me and tried to shove her head under my arm and climb onto my lap.

"Urrrrrgh," I grumbled. "Why are you so crazy?"

Dad crouched down next to me and patted Jeopardy. She put her front paws on his shoulders so it looked like they were hugging. "Aww, poor dog," Dad said. "She just wants to play with you."

"Well, I'm *busy*," I said. I shoved *Ender's Game* between my Lemony Snicket books and *The BFG*. I'd given up on alphabetizing them.

"Maybe she just needs a walk," Dad suggested.

"I have to take her to that class again tomorrow night," I said. "I think that's more than enough bonding time with Jeopardy."

"OK," Dad said, ruffling Jeopardy's fur. He could tell I was not in the best mood. "I'll take her, then." He scooped her up and carried her to the door, which always looks funny because she's got all this fluff and her confused face pokes out over the top.

"OK. Thanks," I said, feeling a little bad. But I got a lot more done while she was gone. All my books were on the shelf and I'd actually managed to find a whole box of real desk stuff by the time she came tearing back up the stairs again.

She was a little calmer after her walk. But I knew it wouldn't last. I knew the Wednesday night class was coming, and I was dreading it. What spectacular new way would Jeopardy find to embarrass me now?

CHAPTER 10

This time when I got to the dog place, only Parker and Merlin were there ahead of me. Parker was practicing "sit" with Merlin, while Alicia set up the equipment with Parsnip bouncing around her feet. I would have hung out against the wall, pretending to read the notices on the bulletin board, but Jeopardy literally dragged me over to the golden retriever.

Merlin wagged his tail when he saw us, and then Parker looked up and smiled in kind of the same way as his dog.

"Hey," he said, holding out his hand so Jeopardy could sniff it. Jeopardy let him pet her for a moment, then ducked under his hand to go sniff Merlin. They circled each other for a minute, trying to sniff each other's butts.

I felt awkward. I didn't have anything to say to Parker, and he didn't seem to have anything to say to me either. We stood there watching our dogs for a minute.

"How long have you had Jeopardy?" Parker asked.

"About a year," I said. "What about you and Merlin?"

He counted on his hand. "Like four weeks, I think—more or less—since just before school started."

"Wow," I said. "I thought you must have had him forever."

"He's pretty attached to me, I guess," Parker said with a laugh. "Like Jeopardy is to you." He didn't seem to mind the idea the way I did. I wondered if Merlin followed him around and pestered him the way Jeopardy stuck with me all the time.

Eric appeared in the doorway, but as we watched him, he took two steps forward and then jerked to a halt, nearly falling backward. He turned around and went, "Meatball! Come *on*!" He tugged on the leash, then leaned back and tried to drag the bulldog in behind him. No luck. I tried not to laugh.

"Sorry, my fault!" we heard Rebekah call from the office on the other side of the door. She came in with Noodles in her arms and Meatball instantly trotted in beside her, gazing longingly up at the fluffy puppy. Eric sighed in exasperation and followed them over to us.

The others arrived right after that, and Alicia had us work on "sit" for five minutes. Then she told us to try "stay."

"This might help some of you with the agility part, too," she said, looking at me. I could feel my cheeks turning red. "Watch. Parsnip, sit." Parsnip planted his little black butt on the floor. His pink tongue hung out as he beamed up at Alicia. "All right. Parsnip, stay." Alicia held out her hand with the palm flat toward Parsnip. She left him there and came over to me.

"Let's try that with Jeopardy," she said. Parsnip watched us, but never moved from his spot. "Have you worked on 'stay' at all?" she asked me.

"Uh," I said. "Maybe Dad has."

Alicia held out a treat. "Sit." Jeopardy gave her a weird look like, *Who do you think you are?* but she sat.

"All right," Alicia said. "Now stay." She put her palm out flat toward Jeopardy and took a step back, then another.

Jeopardy practically rolled her eyes. She gave me a sideways look like, *Seriously? Does she think this is hard?*

"Good. You try," Alicia said, taking the leash from me. Jeopardy stood up as I walked around to face her.

"Jeopardy, sit," I said. She gave Alicia a concerned expression and slowly lowered her butt to the floor. "Now *stay*." I made the same hand gesture as Alicia and took a step back. Jeopardy didn't move. I stepped back again, and then again. She stayed perfectly.

"Great!" Alicia said. "Try that at the hurdles — tell her to stay before you tell her to jump."

Everyone practiced "stay" for a while. Ella held Yeti's leash while Heidi walked away, and Heidi held Trumpet's for her. Eric and Rebekah did the same thing for each other, and so did Parker and Danny. I was the only one working with the teacher. I felt pretty stupid, but Jeopardy showed off her smartness by staying when she was told.

Of course Meatball was the best at staying, though. Eric had a lot more trouble getting him to move than to stay. As soon as his butt was planted, Meatball seemed happy to never get up again. He panted loudly and went *SNOOOOOOOORG* and gazed wistfully at Noodles.

Merlin, on the other hand, didn't love "stay." He

wanted to follow Parker whenever Parker walked away, but he got the hang of it eventually.

Finally Alicia brought us over to the shiny blue tunnel I'd seen at the last class. It was made of thin plastic-y canvas that went *slish slish* when the dogs' tails wagged against it. It was about six feet long, with coils inside the canvas so it could fold up like a slinky, and the opening was as high as Jeopardy's head. Jeopardy's ears perked up, which made me nervous. I wrapped her leash around my hand a bit more firmly.

"The word you'll use here is 'tunnel,'" Alicia said. She made a hand gesture like the one at the hurdles, waving toward the tunnel. "Parsnip, tunnel!" Parsnip immediately sprinted through the tunnel and popped out the other side, wagging his tail.

"Whee!" Rosie yelled. "That's so awesome! I want to do it!" Buttons leaped and spun around at the end of her pink leash like she was thinking, *Me too! Me too!*

"All right, go for it," Alicia said. "I'll wait at the other end of the tunnel." She didn't say it, but I could hear the rest of that sentence in my head: *In case anyone makes a run for it . . . JEOPARDY.*

Rosie unclipped Buttons's leash, flapped her hands

at the tunnel, and hollered, "Buttons, TUNNEL!" The poodle puppy flew into the tunnel, tiny white ears bouncing, and burst out the other end two seconds later.

Alicia held out her hands and went, "Good girl!" but Buttons had already turned around and was racing back through the tunnel to Rosie.

"Yay!" Rosie said, crouching down. "Yay Buttons! Good—" Buttons skidded to a stop just out of Rosie's reach, spun around, and ran back through the tunnel again. "Buttons!" Rosie yelled.

Alicia was ready this time. She scooped Buttons up as soon as the puppy poked her nose out of the tunnel and brought her back around to Rosie. "Some dogs really love the tunnel," Alicia said with a smile.

"You bad thing," Rosie said to Buttons, kissing the puppy's nose.

"OK, but next time you have to use the proper hand motions," her older brother Carlos said bossily. "She has to learn it the *right* way."

"I'M DOING IT JUST FINE!" Rosie yelled.

Parker went next. Merlin stood at the entrance to the tunnel and peered into it. He looked back at Parker like, *Um . . . this doesn't seem like a good idea.*

"Go on, tunnel!" Parker said encouragingly.

Merlin took a step backward. He looked up at Parker again.

"Here," Alicia said, hooking her fingers in Merlin's collar. "You go down to the other end and call him. That should work for this guy."

Parker ran to the other end of the tunnel and crouched down to look through it. Merlin got up on his back legs and leaned toward him around the tunnel, pawing at the air. Then he realized he could see Parker through the tunnel, so he went back to all fours and peered at him.

"Come here, Merlin!" Parker called. "Tunnel!"

Alicia let go of his collar and Merlin bolted through the tunnel, throwing himself at Parker when he reached the other end. Parker tipped over backward, laughing, and wrestled him off.

Noodles jumped into the tunnel right away and then sat down just inside the entrance, panting and looking out at Rebekah with her cute fluffy ears flopped forward. Rebekah threw a treat over her head and Noodles got up to follow it further into the tunnel, then came back to the beginning again. When Rebekah went around to the other end, Noodles came out the front end and followed her around the outside. Alicia had to step in and hold her like she'd held Merlin, but finally Noodles trotted through the whole tunnel to where Rebekah was waiting at the other end. She climbed onto Rebekah's shoulder and licked her face, wriggling happily.

Yeti put one paw inside the tunnel and it rolled a little sideways, rustling. Yeti jumped back and barked at it, one short deep bark, which of course made Jeopardy go "ARF ARF ARF ARF ARF!" Yeti looked over his shoulder at Jeopardy with a bewildered expression like, *Wait, what are you yelling about? Do you know something I don't?*

I finally got Jeopardy to shut up and sit down, but she didn't even want a treat. She just wanted to stare at the tunnel.

Finally Yeti stuck his nose inside and crawled into the tunnel. There was a long pause. He didn't come out the other end. Heidi ran around and stuck her head inside the other end of the tunnel. She started laughing.

"What are you doing, goofy dog?" she cried. "Taking a nap in the middle of class?" Yeti had flopped down halfway along the tunnel. His giant furry paws stretched out behind him and his big pink tongue flapped as he panted. He blinked at her like, *Oh, I thought this nice shady spot was for me.*

When Heidi finally coaxed Yeti out of the tunnel, Eric tried to get Meatball to go through. But it turned out to be impossible. Meatball sat down in front of the tunnel and looked at it disapprovingly. When Eric ran to the other end and called him, Meatball peered inside, sniffed the blue fabric, and then lay down with his jowls flopped over his front paws. He sighed and closed his eyes.

Eric tried everything—calling him, throwing treats into the tunnel, tugging on his leash, but Meatball was having none of it. He rolled onto his back and offered his stomach to Eric with a look that said, *How about a belly rub instead? That sounds like a much better idea.*

"We'll try again later," Alicia said nicely. "Noah and Jeopardy, come on up. Try leaving her leash on so we can catch her more easily if necessary."

Jeopardy lunged forward, but I had her leash wrapped firmly around my hand, so she just scrabbled at the air for a second. I got her lined up in front of the tunnel. "Sit," I said, holding out a treat. She wiggled impatiently, but finally sat down and looked up at me. "Now *stay*," I said, putting my hand flat in front of her nose. Alicia was braced at the other end of the tunnel. I dropped my end of the leash.

"OK, Jeop—" And she was off. *WHOOSH*, my dog flew through the tunnel. She barreled straight into Alicia, knocked her backward onto the floor, and leaped over her head. Jeopardy raced away, barking like crazy.

"ARF ARF ARF ARF ARF!" she yapped gleefully, leaping over the hurdles at the far end of the room. Her leash hit the poles as she flew over them, knocking them all to the ground. "ARF ARF ARF!"

"Jeopardy!" I started to go after her, but Alicia stopped me.

"Try ignoring her," she suggested. "She wants you to chase her, so try waiting for her instead. We'll keep working on the tunnel with the other dogs. I bet she'll come back once she realizes she's not getting any attention from her behavior."

I was dubious about that, but I sat down on the floor and watched Ella and Trumpet instead of Jeopardy.

"ARF ARF ARF!" Jeopardy yelped from the far corner. I imagined she was shouting, *Nah-nah, look at me! I got away! Ha-ha, you can't catch me! Because you're the worst dog owner ever! Ha ha ha and I'm having all this fun now! You're missing out! Hey, pay attention to me! I'm being SO BAD!*

But I ignored her while everyone else went through the tunnel one more time (except Meatball, who still wouldn't). When I finally looked back over at her, she'd stopped barking and sidled over to within a few feet of me. She was staring at me with a disappointed expression.

"That's what you get," I said, shrugging. "Bad dogs miss their turn at the tunnel and don't get treats."

She came a few steps closer, tilting her head. I rested my elbows on my knees and watched Yeti try to roll the tunnel with his nose.

I felt a small nose poke under my arm. Jeopardy lay down next to me and rested her head on my knee. She sighed through her nose, as if she was thinking she should know better than to expect any excitement from me.

I wrapped her leash around my hand and patted her soft, silky head. I have to admit I was pretty surprised she had come back to me. It made me like her a tiny bit more. Maybe she wasn't trying to torture me . . . maybe she really just wanted to play.

But if that was true, why couldn't she play like a *normal* dog? Why couldn't she use her giant brain on being *good* instead of bad?

CHAPTER 11

After the tunnel, Alicia showed us something called the "weave poles." She said in competitions there would be a lot more poles, like six or even twelve, but we'd start out with three. The poles came up to my waist and were made of the same sturdy white pipes as the hurdles, except these had blue stripes instead of green. They were set about a foot apart, all of them stuck into one long white pole at the bottom.

"This is one of the hardest obstacles for dogs to learn," Alicia said. "So be very patient with them! I'm just going to demonstrate how it works tonight, and then we can all try working on it next week."

She had Parsnip stay at one end of the weave poles. Then she said "Weave!" and waved her hand forward. Parsnip jumped to his paws and trotted through the poles. He went to the right of the first pole, then between the poles so he could go to the left of the second pole, then back through to go to the right of the last pole. It was kind of like threading a shoelace on a sneaker.

It looked cool, actually.

"Wow!" Danny cried. "Will Buttons be able to do that?"

"That's the plan," Alicia said with a smile. Parsnip ran over and leaped into Alicia's arms, wagging his tail.

"Of course Buttons will," Heidi said. "She's a little smarty-pants, just like Jeopardy. Right, cutie?" She crouched down to rumple the puppy's fur. Buttons pounced on Heidi's hands and started licking them.

After that, Alicia split us into smaller groups so we could work on the hurdles some more. She put Merlin and Yeti in one group at the tallest hurdle, Buttons, Noodles, and Meatball at the lowest hurdle, and Jeopardy and Trumpet at the medium-height one.

Jeopardy blinked at Trumpet. The beagle wrinkled her forehead. It looked like she was frowning. Ella looked pretty skeptical about me, too.

"I'll go first," she said. "Um . . . OK?"

I nodded, and she unclipped Trumpet. Jeopardy

immediately stood up, but I kept a firm grip on her leash.

"Come on, Trumpet," Ella said, holding the treat in front of her. "Over, Trumpet, over."

Trumpet pawed at her nose for a moment, looking bored.

"Trumpet!" Ella said more firmly. She made the sweeping hand motion. "Over!"

The beagle looked from the treat to Ella's face. Her eyes were huge and soft and brown. They made her look like she was always thinking, *Why me?*

"Over!" Ella said again.

"Ooorrwrrrorrwwwrooorrrr," Trumpet answered mournfully. She got up and shook herself. Her silky brown ears flapped as she stepped deliberately over the bar.

"Good girl!" Ella said, beaming, and Trumpet wagged her tail.

"All *right*, Jeopardy," I said as my dog lunged toward the hurdle. "It's your turn, calm down."

"Don't let go of her leash," Ella reminded me. Her fingers were tapping against her jeans, the way she always tapped on her desk during class.

"Yeah, believe me, I know," I said. "Jeopardy, sit.

Stay." Jeopardy was quivering with anticipation. Her fur trembled as she leaned toward the hurdle. I took my hand away from her nose. "OK, Jeopardy—"

But she'd already sprung to her paws and leaped over the hurdle. My grip on the leash kept her from running away, but she danced at the end of it, trying to get to the other hurdles.

I was so frustrated I felt like kicking over the hurdle. I tugged Jeopardy back around next to me.

"I have an idea," Ella said. She flipped her brown hair over her shoulder. "I mean, if you want to hear it."

"I'll take anything," I said. Jeopardy put one paw on my foot and looked up at me with her bright black eyes.

"I think she thinks you're letting her go when you say 'OK,'" Ella said slowly. "You do it every time—you start with 'OK, Jeopardy,' and she thinks that means 'Go!' before you even get to the real command."

"I do?" I said. "I do that?"

Ella shrugged. "So far. From what I've seen. Try starting with 'over' instead of saying her whole name and all that."

"Do you want to go first?" I asked, glancing at Trumpet. The beagle was lying down on the ground with her long brown ears flopped out to either side. She looked ready for a nap.

"No, I want to see what happens," Ella said. Which I guess was nice of her, but it also made me kind of nervous.

I lined Jeopardy up with the hurdle and made her sit on my right side. "Stay," I said, putting my palm flat in front of her. Slowly I took my hand away. She didn't move, although her eyes flicked from the hurdle to me and back again. I stepped a little sideways. She stayed put. I swung my right hand toward the hurdle. "Over!"

Jeopardy bounded forward and jumped over the hurdle.

"Good girl, Jeopardy!" Ella and I both shouted at the same time. Jeopardy stopped in her tracks and looked back at us, wagging her tail in surprise. Instead of trying to run to the other hurdles, she came trotting back to me and delicately accepted the treat from my hand.

"That was awesome!" I said, crouching to bury my hands in Jeopardy's fur. I gave her a good rub along her sides, and she put her front paws on my shoulders to hug me the way she had with Dad the night before.

"Aw," said Ella, patting Jeopardy's head. "She likes making you happy."

"I can't believe you figured that out," I said. "Thanks for noticing what I was doing wrong." Here I thought *I* was observant. I had no idea I had been confusing Jeopardy like that.

When Alicia said we could try the tunnel again if we wanted to, I took Jeopardy over there. I was more worried about this because I'd have to let her leash go, but I wanted to try Ella's suggestion on the tunnel as well.

Eric came over with Meatball, too. The bulldog ambled slowly behind him and then flopped at his feet as soon as Eric stopped.

"He looks tired out," I said. I couldn't help smiling at Meatball. His big smushy face was hilarious. I liked the way his jowls squished up around his face when he planted his head on the floor. His big brown eyes rolled sideways when he looked mournfully up at Eric, showing the whites of his eyes. Even his snoring was funny. He was just a funny dog.

"I can't imagine *why*," Eric grumbled, looking down at Meatball. "He's hardly done anything! Meatball, you big, lazy oaf."

Snort snorftly snorft, Meatball agreed, licking his chops and slobbering on the floor.

"Want me to wait for Jeopardy at the other end?" Eric offered. "Something tells me this guy's not going anywhere." He poked Meatball gently with the toe of his sneaker.

"Sure," I said. "If you really don't mind—she might run over you."

Eric rubbed his hands together. "I'd like to see her try!" He set Meatball's leash on the floor. The bull-dog barely glanced up as Eric hurried to the other end of the tunnel.

I made Jeopardy sit in front of the tunnel, and again I said "stay" and slowly took my hand away from in front of her nose. She waited, every muscle tensed to run. Finally I waved my hand forward. "Tunnel!"

She was off like a shot. "Good dog!" I shouted, clapping and running along beside the tunnel. "Good *girl*, Jeopardy! Good dog!" She flew out the other end, gave Eric a startled look, and turned around to meet me as I came running up. I held out my arms, meaning to pat her and tell her I was pleased, but to my surprise, she leaped right into them. I stumbled for a second and then stood up with Jeopardy snuggled against my shoulder. She licked my ear and wagged her tail.

I gave her a hug and rubbed her back. I'd never seen her look so pleased.

"Wow, Jeopardy," I said. "Who knew there was a good dog hiding inside you somewhere?"

Jeopardy went "Ruff!" as if to say, *Well, I knew! Sheesh!*

Eric put his hands on his hips and gave Meatball a disapproving look. "Meatball," he said, "why can't you be more like Jeopardy?"

I laughed. "I never thought I'd hear anyone say that," I said.

"Why? Your dog's a genius," Eric said. "Mine's obviously a couch potato. Or maybe just a potato. Until we bring out the skateboard, anyway—you should see him go nuts with that thing." He went over to try to bribe Meatball into going through the tunnel just once.

Jeopardy looked into my eyes. I wasn't sure Eric would really want a "genius" dog if he knew how crazy she acted all the time. Her clever little face just made her look like she was always plotting something sinister . . . which she probably was.

I was happy that she'd done the hurdles and the tunnel right for once. But there was still a part of me that felt like I'd trade her for Meatball in a heartbeat.

Owning a supersmart dog was definitely not all it was cracked up to be.

CHAPTER 12

It was on Thursday that I had my "Eureka!" moment.

Mr. Peary was talking about plants in science. I felt bad because I could tell he was a good teacher; he was really excited about every subject and he made us all get involved. If I didn't already know the difference between plants and fungi, I'd probably have been excited, too.

Instead I pushed an eraser around on my desk, pretending it was a soccer ball and my pencil was Victor dribbling the ball down the field. Another pencil stood guard at the goal made by two books on the other side of the desk.

Mr. Peary stopped drawing on the whiteboard and started handing out a work sheet about botany. He started with Maggie, so by the time he got around to me, everyone was bent over their papers, working. I hid the eraser in my desk and rearranged the books, trying to look like I was paying attention.

Mr. Peary gave a work sheet to Ella and then crouched beside my desk. "You got a perfect score on the quiz yesterday, Noah," he said in a low voice. "Great work. Did you already cover this section in your previous school?"

"Um . . . yeah," I mumbled. "It was a different book, but kinda the same stuff."

"Maybe you can help me get ready for the next section, then," he said. "Animals and cells and things. Did you already study that?"

I shook my head. Mr. Peary took a spiral-bound book from his desk and handed it to me. It said TEACHER ACTIVITY GUIDE across the top. Whoa. I'd never looked inside the teacher's book before.

"While the others fill out the work sheet, I'd like you to check out the activities in the next chapter. See if there's anything you think would be fun. I want stuff we can get up and do, instead of me just talking at you guys all the time." Mr. Peary grinned. It was like he had read my mind. It made me kind of nervous. "And we don't have to do exactly what's in there, either. If you think we could change any of these ideas to make them more interesting, just let me know."

He handed me a stack of Post-its and went back to his desk. I flipped to the Animal Kingdom section of the guide. It started with stuff about jellyfish and starfish and then went on to insects and reptiles and finally mammals. There were activities about animal camouflage, different shapes of bird beaks, building models of cells out of candy, metamorphosis, endangered species, and pesticides. A lot of the experiments sounded so cool, I wanted to try them right away. I stuck Post-its all over the place with little notes scribbled on them about how I thought we could do them.

I got so interested, I didn't even notice that a whole hour had passed until the bell rang and Mr. Peary said it was time for PE. Was this what it was like to be a teacher? I always thought it was just grading homework and talking about fractions and giving quizzes.

I never thought about trying to make lessons more fun. I hadn't ever imagined planning field trips and making up games for the class and figuring out new ways to learn something that could be boring in a book, but exciting when you did it in real life, like finding planets through a real telescope or folding different shapes of paper airplanes to see which one went the farthest.

Maybe I would be a good teacher one day. I wondered if Mr. Peary would let me help him with ideas for the other sections, like social studies or language arts. I really wanted to know if there were teacher activity guides for those, too.

"I didn't finish the whole section," I said, handing the book back to him. "But, uh . . . it's really cool."

"That's OK," said Mr. Peary. "You can keep going through it until the rest of the class is done with the stuff you already know."

I started to follow the rest of the class out the door and then turned back. "Uh, Mr. Peary? Could I—do you have a book like that for social studies, too?"

"Got some ideas for Greek myths?" Mr. Peary asked with a smile.

"Well, kind of . . . um . . . I was just thinking . . . maybe we could act some of them out? Like make our own plays?" I said. "Someone could make the togas, and we could divide into groups and everyone could act out a different myth—"

"That would be awesome!" said a voice behind me. I jumped. I thought everyone else was gone. I wouldn't normally get all excited about school stuff in front of other people. I turned around and saw that Nikos had stopped in the doorway. He came back toward us. "Mr. Peary, my dad could do the food! He makes these stuffed grape leaves that are *amazing*. And can I be on the team that does the Icarus myth? The one about the guy with the wings?"

"And maybe then we could read the Percy Jackson books," I said. "They're all about the Greek gods and myths and everything."

"I love those books!" Nikos said. "My favorite is book two, but I just started book five. Oh, Mr. Peary, I changed my mind—I want to do the story of Prometheus, where he gives humans fire and then the gods punish him by chaining him to a rock where an eagle eats his liver for the rest of eternity."

"Awesome!" I said.

"Boys!" Mr. Peary interrupted. "I'm glad you're so excited about this, but you'd better get to PE. Coach Mason won't be happy if you're late."

"OK," Nikos said. "But you'll think about it?"

Mr. Peary shook his head, smiling. "I'm going to regret saying this, but—it sounds like fun. I'll think about it."

"Yeah!" Nikos whooped. "Come on, Noah." He led the way out the door and talked to me about Percy Jackson and The 39 Clues all the way to the outdoor field. I found out his parents actually grew up in Greece, which I could have guessed from his name. He liked the same video games I did. By the time we joined the others stretching, I'd decided this was the best day so far at my new school.

Nikos caught up to me while we ran around the track and introduced me to his friend Teddy, the one I'd seen him running with on Tuesday. Teddy was half Taiwanese and he was in Miss Woodhull's class. He seemed smart like Nikos.

"Noah's already done most of the stuff we're working on in class right now," Nikos said to Teddy.

"Man, you must be bored," Teddy said, wiping his wrist across his forehead. "I always feel like class is going *so* slowly, and I haven't even done it all before. It makes me want to jump around and act crazy just to get things moving."

That's when it hit me.

Me doodling and daydreaming and building stuff on my desk was exactly like Jeopardy hiding my things and running around the dog place and barking and staring at me all the time. She was acting crazy because she was frustrated with how slow everything was.

Jeopardy wasn't a bad dog. She was *bored*.

CHAPTER 13

I thought about my theory all through PE. It made sense. On the days when I took her to class, Jeopardy was calmer afterward. She'd fall asleep instead of running around the house, because she'd used up her energy thinking so hard in class. But on Tuesday she'd been a lunatic as usual because we hadn't done anything to use her brain. It made her bored and restless.

She must be following me around because she was hoping I'd give her something to do, like Mr. Peary had given me something to keep me from being bored in class.

"Hey," Teddy said to me as we jogged back from the field. "Wanna sit with me and Nikos at lunch? We're entering this invention contest, but we could use some help with our idea."

"Sure!" I said. I'd never heard of an invention contest. I wondered what the prize was. Maybe I could invent something to keep dogs from getting bored, like a game Jeopardy could play by herself if we weren't around.

At the end of the day, Nikos waved to me as I got in my mom's car, and so did Rory. Mom gave me a pleased look and I shrugged. "Don't get too excited," I said. "They'll probably forget my name again by tomorrow."

"Uh-huh," Mom said. Jeopardy went "Ruff!" and I leaned around to pat her on the head. She nudged my hand with her nose and then licked my fingers.

"Hey, I can still use the basement, right?" I asked. "That's still for me?"

"Of course," Mom said, looking even more pleased. "What do you want it for?"

"Nothing important," I said. "Just an idea I'm working on."

At home I dropped my book bag at the bottom of the stairs and headed through the kitchen to the basement door. Jeopardy followed right behind me. We went down the beige carpeted stairs and looked around the open, empty space at the bottom.

The wall-to-wall carpet was short and thickly woven, with a gray and green pattern on the sandy background so that dirt smudges wouldn't show up.

The walls had dark brown wood paneling and the recessed lights in the ceiling were on a dimmer so I could make them brighter or darker from the door. Sunlight came in through the small windows at the top of the wall all the way around the room. A door in the corner led to the laundry room.

There was nothing in the room yet. Mom and Dad were using the attic for storage, and they told me they wouldn't put anything in the basement until I decided what I wanted to do with it. I walked around the space with Jeopardy at my feet, her brown-and-white fur bouncing as she trotted next to me.

I could ask them for a TV, so I could set up my video games in here, farther away from Violet's screaming in the sunroom. Or if I got straight A's, they might even let me have a Foosball table down here, or Ping-Pong, or something like that.

But for now, I had a better idea.

It took me an hour to find all the things I was looking for. Jeopardy followed me around and barked whenever I picked something up. I gave her a small cushion to carry, and she seized it proudly between her teeth and followed me back down the stairs.

By the time Mom came downstairs to call me for dinner, I was ready.

She stopped on the stairs and blinked several times. "What's going on in here?"

"Watch," I said. "Jeopardy, sit. Now stay." Jeopardy sat and watched me with her ears pricked forward. We'd already tried this a couple of times, so she knew what was coming. I walked up to the first obstacle I'd built, a makeshift hurdle of a yardstick and a couple of books.

"Over!" I called, waving my hand in the right motion. Jeopardy bolted forward. By the time she cleared the hurdle, I was at the tunnel I'd made out of cushions and blankets. "Tunnel!" I yelled, and she raced into it. I ran as fast as I could to the other end, so when she popped out I was there to say "Over!" for the next hurdle I'd built. Jeopardy sailed over that one as well.

"Now sit!" I called, and she promptly sat. I caught up to her and gave her a treat. "Good dog," I said, rubbing her head and grinning at her. She wagged her tail with a self-satisfied expression like, *Well, of course I am*.

Mom started clapping. "That was brilliant!" she said. "You learned all that in class?"

"In class we're still doing the obstacles one at a time," I said. "I figured Jeopardy was ready to put them together."

"Maybe you can rent some of the equipment for the weekend," Mom said. "You know, so the rest of us can have our couch cushions back." She lifted her eyebrows at the tunnel.

"Yeah, OK," I said. I wondered what other equipment Alicia might have.

After dinner I showed Dad and Violet the obstacle course, which was kind of hilarious because Violet wanted to run through it after Jeopardy. She jumped over the hurdles and crawled through the tunnel shrieking, "Wheee! Wheee! I'm a dog, too! Wheeee!" Dad and I couldn't stop laughing.

"If only you were as easily trained as Jeopardy," Dad said, picking Violet up.

"T'ank you for letting me play in it," Violet said sweetly to me. She held out her hands and I let her hug me. I didn't often admit it, but even Violet could be cute sometimes.

The best part was, it totally worked. Jeopardy fell asleep for the rest of the evening, so I could do my homework and unpack boxes in peace while she snoozed on the orange-and-blue rug in my room.

I was even excited for Friday night's class.

I wanted to ask Alicia what other obstacles there

were, so I got there early. Maybe she read my mind or something, because there were brand-new obstacles all over the room. There was a low, flat table, painted bright yellow. There was a small green seesaw. There was something that looked like a triangle or two ramps propped together, so you'd walk up one side and down the other like a tiny mountain. There was even a fake tire hanging between some tall pipes so the dogs could jump through it.

"Hey Noah!" Alicia called. "Check this one out. See what Jeopardy thinks of it." She was crouching beside another blue tunnel, but this one had a piece of fabric attached to the end like a big floppy sock. So instead of seeing the other side when you looked into the tunnel, all you saw was a curtain of material at the end.

"The dog has to push through the chute to get out the other end," Alicia explained. "Sometimes it makes them a little nervous, so I usually hold it open the first couple of times. But she might be ready for it the way it is."

Jeopardy already had her head inside the tunnel. I unclipped her leash and went to the end of the chute. "Come on, Jeopardy!" I called, kneeling on the floor.

The fabric sock started flailing as Jeopardy nudged it with her head. It looked like a blob monster staggering around blindly.

"Here, girl! Come here, Jeopardy!" She followed the sound of my voice, shoving the chute around with her nose until she found the opening at the end. Finally she wriggled free and bounded onto my lap, wagging her tail.

"Good dog!" I said, giving her a treat and scratching behind her ears.

"As I expected," Alicia said with a smile. "She's a natural. You're doing great with her."

I felt weirdly warm and fuzzy after she said that. I thought I was doing so badly with Jeopardy, or at least that she was deliberately messing with me. But now that I could imagine what she felt like, it was easier to figure out what she wanted.

Heidi and Ella and Rebekah arrived before the other guys did and came straight over to me. Noodles promptly tried to pounce on Jeopardy's head. Jeopardy jumped back, barking, and Noodles fled across the room, so Jeopardy chased her, much to the delight of Noodles.

"ROWRF! ROWRF!" Yeti woofed. Heidi unclipped him and he bounded over to join the chase.

He kept losing track of the smaller dogs underneath him, so he'd turn around in circles looking confused while they ran around his paws. Then he blundered backward and got tangled up in the weave poles, so Heidi went over to rescue him.

"You want to play, too, Trumpet?" Ella asked her beagle. Trumpet wrinkled her brow and looked at Ella like, *As if I would ever be that undignified!* She yawned widely and lay down, resting her head on Ella's sneaker. Ella and Rebekah giggled.

"Oh, Noah," Rebekah said in this way-too-casual way. "So, like, we noticed you sat with Nikos again at lunch today." She smiled mischievously and Ella shot her a look that was like, *Don't you dare.*

"Yeah," I said. "He's got this idea for a great invention—"

"Really?" Rebekah interrupted. "Wow, that's cool. So anyway, like . . . so, does he ever say anything about Ella?"

"Rebekah!" Ella squealed. "Shut up! Oh my *gosh*!" She said "oh my *gosh*" exactly the way Heidi always said it, and I wondered which one of them had picked it up from the other. "Don't answer that," Ella said to me. "Ignore her."

"OK," I said with a shrug. I couldn't remember

him saying anything about Ella specifically. Why would he?

There was a funny pause, and then Ella burst out, "I mean, unless he did. Does he? I mean, not that I care, just wondering. Has he? I bet he hasn't. You're right, it's a dumb question. Never mind, I don't want to know."

"Uh . . ." I said, and thankfully at that moment Eric and Parker came in with their dogs, so I was saved from having to figure out the mysterious minds of girls.

Once everyone was there, Alicia walked us around the room and showed us all of the obstacles one at a time. It was crazy; I had no idea there were so many. She told us about agility competitions and how some of them were shown on TV.

"Buttons!" Rosie squealed, scooping up her puppy and hugging her tightly. "You could totally do that! You're going to be on TV! We're going to make you famous!"

"As long as there are no pink ribbons involved," Danny joked.

"RARF!" Buttons yapped as if she was agreeing with him. Everyone laughed except Rosie, who rolled her eyes.

The yellow table was only about a hand's length off the floor and shaped like a big square. The idea was that we were supposed to send the dog onto the table ("Table!") and then make them lie down for thirty seconds, and then call them off again ("Off!"). We hadn't practiced "lie down" yet, so Alicia said we could make them sit instead. Of course, Buttons was already an expert at "lie down," like she was at everything else, so Rosie and Carlos got her to do the whole trick exactly the way Parsnip had.

"Show-offs," Heidi said admiringly. "Who's a star, Buttons?"

"ROWRF!" Yeti barked, like *ME! It's ME! I'm a star! Over here!* The funny part about Yeti on the table was that he barely fit on it. When he was standing on the floor, he could lean over and reach the treat Heidi put on the far side of the table from him. And when she finally got him up onto it, his big white paws flopped off the front and back when he tried to lie down. It looked really goofy, especially with his enormous shaggy grin.

Jeopardy spent half her time on the table sniffing around for treats the other dogs had overlooked, but she went on and off it when I told her to, so I figured that was a good start. She looked pretty cute lying down on the bright yellow background, too.

Meatball was having none of the seesaw. We watched Parsnip run up the ramp, wait in the center while the seesaw tipped slowly underneath him, and then run down the other side and jump off. The seesaw made a small bang when it landed back in its original position. Meatball didn't like that at all. He hunched his shoulders up around his wrinkly head and looked gloomy. Eric tried to drag him over to it, but he dug his paws in and refused to go anywhere near it.

Even Buttons would only go halfway up the seesaw board. She got nervous when it started to tip underneath her and jumped off onto the floor. Alicia said that was OK, because we'd start with modified seesaws first. She showed us how we could put a rolled-up towel under the middle of a flat board, and then when a dog walked along the board, it would tip only a little bit, so they could get used to it. If we stuck around for the advanced class, we'd eventually work our way up to even bigger seesaws than the one she had there.

The mountain ramp thing was called an "A-frame." The peak of it was about level with my chest, so it wasn't too high. Parsnip climbed up one side and scrambled down the other, wagging his tail like he loved being the center of attention.

Alicia showed us how there were painted yellow areas on the bottom of each end. She said in a competition, the dog had to step into that area as it came on and off the A-frame, or it would lose points.

We saw why when Merlin and Yeti went over the A-frame. It was easy for them to jump onto the board above the yellow line and then jump off again from the other side. Yeti practically flew from the top of the A-frame to the floor, he was so excited to get to the treat in Heidi's hand.

It wasn't just big dogs, either; Noodles cleared the whole yellow area when she came down the A-frame, too, and then she bounded over to Rebekah with her little pink tongue hanging out.

Jeopardy was surprisingly good at hitting the yellow spots. I thought she'd be in too much of a hurry to get over the A-frame. But when I put my hand in front of her and said, "Slow," she walked carefully down the other side, stepping deliberately on the yellow part of the board as if she knew exactly what I wanted.

The tire jump was easy to figure out, but it turned out this was one trick Buttons wasn't perfect at. The poodle puppy was so small, she could run right under the tire, between it and the poles holding it up, even when Alicia lowered it almost to the floor. Buttons ran underneath it every time Rosie yelled "Tire!" which was the tire jump word. Rosie tried throwing a treat through the middle of the tire, but Buttons just ran right under it and gobbled up the treat on the other side.

Rosie stamped her foot in frustration as I sent Jeopardy sailing through the tire. "Buttons!" she said. "Be more like Jeopardy!"

There it was again. *Be more like Jeopardy*—now I'd heard it twice in one week. I patted Jeopardy's head, grinning. The world was totally upside down.

CHAPTER 14

After class, Mom came inside with Violet to ask Alicia if we could rent some of the agility stuff for the weekend. Alicia was thrilled to hear that I wanted to practice more at home.

"I think you two could be great at this," she said, crouching to pat Jeopardy's head. "Let's see what's easiest to transport." She showed me how to break down the hurdles and gave me three of those. The tunnel squished up into a flat round hoop, so I could take that, too, plus the chute to attach to it. The A-frame folded in half so it could slide flat into the trunk of our car. And she gave me a short board to use to practice the seesaw trick by putting a rolled-up towel under it.

Heidi and Yeti had been waiting for her mom in the office, but they came back in when she saw us breaking down the equipment and stacking it by the door.

"Whatcha doing?" she asked. Yeti tilted his head

curiously at the pile of hurdle poles. He poked the folded A-frame with his nose and Jeopardy went "RUFF!" like, *Hey! That's mine!*

"Well, uh," I said, rubbing my head. "I thought maybe we'd . . . practice at home." That sounded super-dorky now that I was saying it out loud.

Heidi's face lit up. "That's the best idea ever!" she said. "Oh my gosh, do you have space for all this stuff in your house?"

"Well, the basement—" I started to say, but she kept talking.

"I wanted to practice at home but I tried to get Yeti to jump over a book on the floor and he got so excited that he kept running and knocked this crazy fancy-looking clock off the table with his tail and then he had to go hide under my bed for half an hour because we were afraid my mom would be really mad but it ended up OK because apparently she never liked it anyway and it wasn't as expensive as it looked but she still said we shouldn't practice inside the house except it's getting kind of cold for practicing outside and anyway it's more fun with the right equipment, right?"

"Uh," I said. "Sure."

"So you can put all this in your basement? Oh my gosh, you guys are going to be so much better than the rest of us by Monday! I mean, you are already, so I guess you'll be, like, practically ready for competition after practicing."

"Oh, I don't—" I started to say, but then Parker came back inside with Eric.

"My dad's not here yet," Parker said, rubbing his arms. "We figured we'd wait in here." Meatball flopped down on the floor and made his snoozing snort noises.

"Guess what?" Heidi said. "Noah's taking some of the stuff home to practice over the weekend!"

Now I was really embarrassed. It was like I'd signed up to do extra credit for no reason or something.

But Parker looked as interested as Heidi. "I didn't know you could do that!" he said. Merlin wagged his tail and came over to see what Yeti was sniffing inside the scrunched-up tunnel.

"Well," I said, "I mean, if you guys want to come over and practice, too . . . "

"Really?" Heidi yelped. "Are you serious? You wouldn't mind?"

"I have to ask my dad, but I could probably come over tomorrow around noon," Parker said.

"Can Danny come, too?" Heidi asked. "Ella would, but she has her cousin's bat mitzvah."

"Uh—sure," I said, realizing I should probably run this by my mom first. I looked over my shoulder and saw her talking to Alicia. Violet sat on one end of the seesaw, bellowing about how someone should sit on the other end for her.

"What about you?" Parker asked Eric.

Eric hunched his shoulders and looked down at the floor. "Um," he said. "Well, like, I—I kind of have plans."

Parker lifted his eyebrows. "Plans? You never have plans."

"I do sometimes!" Eric said. "I'm, uh—going to the movies."

"OOOOOOOHHHHHHH," Parker and Heidi said at the same time.

Heidi started laughing. "Bet I can guess with who!" she said. Eric rubbed his hand through his hair and squirmed.

"Meatball's terrible at this anyway," he said. "All the practice in the world isn't going to help him."

SNOOOOOORGH, agreed Meatball without opening his eyes.

Eric sighed. "I don't know why *I* have to have the most embarrassing dog in the world."

I couldn't believe it. Those were almost the exact words I'd thought about Jeopardy! I'd never guessed that Eric was embarrassed. I was too busy thinking about how crazy *my* dog was. His dog was just funny, and besides, he already had lots of friends. He had nothing to be embarrassed about.

It was kind of weird . . . I felt like the story of my life had been flipped around and recast with someone else in my part.

"So I guess Rebekah's busy, too," Heidi said, grinning mischievously. "So it'd just be me and Parker and Danny. Is that OK, Noah?"

"Uh—let me check with my mom," I said.

To my relief, Mom said yes. I gave them all my phone number and address, and they said they'd be there around noon.

"Great!" Mom said, smiling from ear to ear. "I'll make lunch!"

I herded her out the door before she had a heart attack from how excited she was. The only bad part was this totally made her feel like she was right to sign me up for the agility class. I hate it when she's right about stuff like that, but at least she didn't rub it in on the way home.

We spent the rest of the night getting the house ready for visitors. While Mom and Dad tidied up the living room, I finished unpacking my room. There were a lot of things that still didn't have a place, so I shoved them all in one box and hid that in the closet. But I found some of my favorite T-shirts stuffed around a couple of photo frames in a bag of nice clothes that I wouldn't otherwise have unpacked for months, so that made me pretty happy.

Dad helped me set up the agility equipment in the basement. We built a whole obstacle course down there. It looked even cooler than I expected. I made a table out of an enormous red, white, and blue square pillow, and I printed out photos of dogs that looked like Yeti, Buttons, Merlin, Meatball, Noodles, Trumpet, and Jeopardy to pin up on the walls.

Jeopardy followed us around while we put everything together. She poked the hurdles with her nose and jumped back in surprise when the bar fell down. She ran through the tunnel about six times. She put her front paws up on the A-frame and leaned up to sniff the top of it, checking for overlooked treats. She walked over the mini seesaw board and barked at it when it tipped underneath her.

Finally she settled down on the table-cushion and fell fast asleep.

I sat down next to her and stroked her long, soft fur. She opened her eyes and turned her head to rest it on my knee, and then fell asleep again. After a moment, she wriggled onto her back so all four little white paws were in the air and I could rub her chest and belly.

Her long nose and alert ears looked extra cute when she was asleep. A genius *and* cute—who knew?

I just hoped that Saturday would go OK. I hoped Jeopardy would be good, and everyone would have fun, and nothing terrible would happen. My stomach jumped nervously as I looked around the room. I was having new people over for the first time.

What if it was a total disaster?

CHAPTER 15

Jeopardy could tell I was nervous the next morning. She kept running to the door and barking, which made me freak out and run after her, only to find out there was nobody there. This happened *four times*. Finally I took her into the yard to chase a Frisbee while we waited. It was too stressful to keep checking out the door every two minutes.

I threw the neon yellow disc and worried. What if nobody came? What if they were all playing a joke on me? What if something better came along and they just forgot to tell me they weren't coming?

"Noah!" my mom called from the kitchen door. "Parker and Merlin are here!"

"Come on, Jeopardy!" I called. She ran up to me with the Frisbee in her teeth. She was holding it upside down so she could get a grip on it, which made it stick up in the air like a neon yellow dinner plate. I wrestled it out of her mouth and we hurried into the kitchen.

Parker was sitting at the table in the dining room, eating some of the carrot sticks my mom had left out for us. Merlin sniffed around the walls eagerly. He looked up when we came in and barked. Jeopardy bounded over to him and put her front paws on his back. Merlin went "RRRRFF!" and rolled away from her. Soon they were wrestling under the chairs and all over the dark blue-and-gold area rug.

Parker laughed. "Boy, Merlin loves other dogs," he said.

"Yeah, so does Jeopardy," I said, "once she's used to them."

Parker started telling me about how he got Merlin and how the golden retriever used to escape from the yard and follow him to school. He was describing this crazy food fight Merlin sort of started when the doorbell rang.

"ARF ARF ARF ARF ARF ARF ARF!" Jeopardy announced frantically, spinning around and looking at me like, *QUICK! DO SOMETHING!*

"Wow," I said to Parker as my mom went to get the door. "I don't think we ever had a food fight at my school in Rochester."

"That might be the last one we ever have!" Parker said. "We had to clean it up and it was *so* gross!"

A small bundle of white fluff shot into the room and zoomed around the furniture. Jeopardy and Merlin both looked startled, then dropped to the floor to watch Buttons zip through the chair legs.

"Man, Rosie threw a fit when I asked to take Buttons today," Danny said, shaking his head as he walked into the room. He was wearing a Miami Dolphins jersey and jeans. "She was all: 'NO! *MY* DOG! ONLY I CAN PLAY WITH HER!' until Mom offered to take her shopping with Pippa instead. I mean, come *on*. She's going to come home with, like, seven new pink outfits to cheer her up. Does that sound fair?"

"Uh-oh," I said, nodding at his football shirt. "Don't let my dad catch you in that. The Dolphins are our arch-nemesis."

Danny looked down at his jersey in confusion. "Oh," he said, "my grandpa gave me this. I didn't even think about it. Why, who's your team?"

"The Buffalo Bills," I said.

"I saw them play the Jets a few weeks ago," Danny said. "The Bills totally dominated them."

"I was *at* that game!" I said. "Me and my friend Josh!"

"No way!" Danny said. He started telling me

about all the games he'd been to in person. It turned out Parker liked baseball better than football, but Danny would watch any sport except volleyball, which he thought was too boring.

The three dogs ran around our feet while we talked and ate grapes and carrots and crackers with cheese and this chickpea dip my mom makes. I didn't even notice that Heidi was twenty minutes late until she got there.

"I'm sorry!" she said as she unclipped Yeti. "We were getting ready to go and then Yeti stepped in his water dish and it startled him so much he knocked over his food dish, too, so there was wet kibble everywhere and my mom had to go lie down in a dark room while we cleaned it up because we gave her such a headache. It is so weird having someone in the house who makes a bigger mess than I do!" She hugged Yeti with a big smile and he licked her ear affectionately.

Heidi's messy reddish-blond hair was clipped back with a brown dachshund-shaped barrette, but most of it was falling loose already. Her corduroys had a green-and-blue flower pattern on them, so at first it was hard to tell that the grass stains on the knees weren't part of the design.

After the dogs had all sniffed one another for an eternity, I took everyone downstairs to the basement.

"Wow!" Heidi yelled when I turned the lights on. "This looks amazing!"

"You should leave it like this all the time!" said Parker. He walked between the hurdles and whistled. "Boy, *I* kind of want to run through it when it looks like this!"

"Me too!" Danny shouted. He leaped over two of the hurdles and threw himself onto the table-cushion. I decided not to tell him my three-year-old sister had done the same thing.

"Danny, sit!" Heidi said, laughing, and he sat up with his hands together like paws.

Buttons galloped over and leaped onto the cushion with him. Her tiny pom-pom of a tail wagged as she tried to scramble onto his lap. Danny fell over backward and let her stand on his chest and lick his chin.

"Jeopardy's all ready to go," Parker pointed out. My dog was standing at the mouth of the tunnel, watching me expectantly. Merlin nosed her in the side and she gave him an impatient *Can't you see I'm working here?* look.

"Jeopardy, stay!" I said, walking over to her. Her paws danced on the carpet and her mouth opened into a kind of dog smile. I made her wait another ten seconds, and then I swung my hand toward the tunnel. "Tunnel!" I yelled.

She disappeared into it like a flash. I ran to the other end and waved my hand at the A-frame when she popped out. "A-frame!" I called, and she zipped up one side and down the other.

"Now over! Over! Over!" I said, steering her through the hurdles. "And table!"

"AAAAAAAAH!" Danny yelled as Jeopardy took a flying leap onto his chest and sent Buttons tumbling off the cushion on the other side. Jeopardy sat down with her tail flopping into Danny's face and gave me a triumphant expression. Heidi literally fell over laughing.

"All right, I know when I've been beaten," Danny said through a mouthful of Jeopardy's fur. Buttons jumped around Jeopardy's paws, trying to get up to lick her face.

"She claims this territory for the kingdom of Jeopardy!" Heidi teased, nudging Danny with her foot.

"Come on, Merlin, you can do that, too!" Parker said. "Tunnel!"

Merlin stuck his nose inside the tunnel, then came back out to look doubtfully at Parker.

"Go on, tunnel!" Parker said, throwing a treat inside. As Merlin went in to get it, Parker ran to the other end. But before he got there, Merlin popped out the front end again and followed him around the outside. Parker didn't notice until he stuck his head inside the tunnel and went, "Hey, where'd he go?" Merlin poked his damp black nose into Parker's neck and Parker jumped back with a startled yelp.

"Oh, poor Yeti," Heidi said, ruffling her dog's fur. The huge shaggy dog had one paw on the seesaw board, tipping it up and down over the rolled-up towel. He tried cautiously to stand on one end, but his giant paws barely fit on the narrow yellow board.

"Let's try the hurdles, Yeti," Heidi said. "Come on, over! Over!" Yeti agreeably followed her to the hurdles and plowed straight through them again. Even when he managed to step over one with his front paws, it was like he forgot before his back paws got there, so they always hit the bar.

"Goofy!" Heidi said, setting the bars back up. "Here, try again. Watch the treat." She held it in front of Yeti's nose, then tossed it over the hurdle. Yeti promptly knocked the bar over again getting to it. *Chomp chomp chomp*, he went, munching the treat cheerfully.

"Try setting the bar higher," I suggested, showing her how to adjust the height. "He's so big, he probably doesn't even notice it. Maybe if it's higher up, he'll pay more attention to it."

"Great idea!" Heidi said. "Yeti! Over!"

It totally worked. Yeti walked up to the hurdle and then looked down at the bar in surprise, like, *Hey, where'd that come from? What's it doing there?* He shook his head so his long black ears flapped, and then he hopped right over the hurdle and scarfed up the treat on the other side.

"Yaaaaayy!" Heidi squealed, clapping her hands. "Good boy! Good dog!"

Jeopardy came running over to make sure no one else was getting any treats without her. Buttons was right behind her, yapping with excitement.

"Want to see something cool?" Danny said, sitting up. "Carlos has started teaching Buttons to do 'shake.'

Check it out." He came over, crouched beside the poodle, and held out his hand. "Buttons, shake!"

The puppy sniffed at his hand with her little black button nose.

"Come on, shake!" Danny said again. Buttons put one paw into his hand, and then immediately put the other paw on there as well and leaned up toward him, wagging her tail.

"Aww, too cute," Heidi said, picking up Buttons and snuggling her into her neck. Buttons seized a lock of Heidi's hair in her mouth and shook it, going "Rrrrr! Rrrrr!"

"Yes, you are very fierce," Heidi said, touching Buttons' nose with her own. The puppy tried to grab Heidi's nose in her teeth and Heidi ducked away, giggling.

We practiced with the dogs on the equipment for about an hour, although Jeopardy was the only one who paid close attention for the whole time. She never took her eyes off me when I had a treat in my hand or pointed myself at an obstacle. She was always ready to go.

Finally we took a break when Mom came down with chicken salad sandwiches and celery sticks and glasses of grape juice for everyone. She didn't even say anything about not spilling grape juice on the carpet, which was cool of her. Although perhaps she would have if she knew Heidi better. But even Heidi managed not to spill anything.

"Oh my gosh, I almost forgot!" Heidi said. She pulled a scrap of paper out of her pocket. "Ella said Nikos wanted to call you but he didn't have your number. So I said I'd give you his. Something about working on an invention tomorrow?"

"Oh, cool," I said, taking the paper from her. It was wrinkled and crumpled and had half a gummi bear stuck to it, but I could still read the phone number scribbled in pencil. "I'll call him."

I was glad Heidi didn't ask me anything about Ella and Nikos. She didn't act like she cared about that kind of thing.

I threw out the gummi bear, smoothed the paper, and put it in my pocket, trying not to smile too much. I wanted to look like I was too cool to get excited about having someone to hang out with, but secretly I was kind of psyched that Nikos wanted me to call him.

Then Heidi said, "Hey you guys, want to go to the park later? Rory was trying to set up a game, maybe soccer or Frisbee?"

"Frisbee!" Danny shouted. "And dibs I get Noah on my team! I called him!"

"Not fair!" Heidi said. "Rory's going to want him on *her* team, and if we put the three of you together, there's no way the rest of us could win."

"Seriously!" Parker said. "We all know how good he is!"

"I'm not *that*—" I started to say.

"I bet you're faster than either Brett or Luis," said Parker.

"Blech, and you're nicer than Brett," Heidi said, making a face. "Plus you catch a Frisbee better than Luis. And way better than me! Danny, I should get to be on Noah's team, because I'm so terrible."

"Too bad, I called him," Danny said, lying back on the pillow again with a satisfied smirk.

"Well, you can fight Rory for him, then," Heidi said with a grin. "*That* should be fun to watch!" She turned to me. "I'm much better at soccer than Frisbee," she said. "I swear I am. Do you play soccer?"

"I have, sure," I said. I felt weird and smiley, like giant birds were spreading their wings inside me. Even back in Rochester, I couldn't remember people fighting to have me on their team before. They wouldn't do that if they didn't like me, right? Danny must already think of me as a friend . . . and maybe Rory did, too.

Jeopardy came over and climbed on my lap, staring into my face like, *Why have we stopped? I can jump more hurdles! I really can!* Then she got distracted by the rest of my sandwich on the plate beside me and tried to flop over my lap to get to it. I moved it out of reach and put my arms around her. She rested her head on my arm with a contented sigh and I patted her side with my other hand.

It was hard to believe, but in one week, mostly thanks to Jeopardy, I'd gone from having no friends at all to having almost too many friends.

If it weren't for my dog, I would never have met Heidi, and I definitely wouldn't have been in that class with Danny and Parker and the others. Now here I was, hanging out with Heidi and Danny and Parker just like I used to hang out with Victor and Josh and Anjali, only this time there were a lot more dogs involved.

Then later we'd see Rory, and tomorrow I'd go work on an invention with Nikos and Teddy. I had plenty of people to sit with at lunch, and a million things to talk to them about.

Not only that, but I'd solved the mystery of why

my dog acted so weird all the time. Now that we had stuff to do together, she wouldn't be so bored—and she wouldn't drive me so crazy.

Maybe it wasn't so bad having a smarty-pants dog.

Maybe it was actually pretty cool.

Tombo is a great dog . . . when
he isn't getting into trouble!

Pet Trouble

Bad to the Bone Boxer

Turn the page for a sneak peek!

Pet Trouble

We went straight out to the animal shelter that afternoon. I was so excited all the way there. This was going to change everything. Now I would have a dog and Rosie would have a dog and Pippa would just have her big, lazy cat. Rosie and I could take our dogs to the park together. She'd call me so our dogs could play with each other, and this time she'd forget to call Pippa instead. I'd have my best friend back.

Plus a dog! I didn't even care what kind we got. A dog is a dog, right? They run and play and lick your face and sleep on the couch. Easy and fun. That's what I figured.

"We're getting a dog!" I said, poking Deandre's shoulder.

"Ow," he said. "And yeah, I know. My ears do work, you realize."

"I had a corgi when I was your age, Michelle," Mom said to me.

"We always had mutts," Dad said. "Loulou was the first purebred dog I ever owned."

Loulou was a retired racing greyhound Mom and Dad adopted soon after they got married. There are photos of me with her when I was two and Deandre was six, but I don't remember her. She was a really pretty dog, all long legs and a long elegant snout.

"Maybe we'll get another greyhound," Deandre said.

"We'll see what's available," Mom said as we pulled into the Wags to Whiskers parking lot. "It'll probably be mostly mutts here, but that's OK. Your father and I think it's very important to adopt a dog from a shelter."

"So we can give it a good home!" I said. "Poor abandoned dog!"

The woman at the front desk was thrilled to meet us. Her name was Miss Hameed, and she had long dark hair coiled up in a thick bun on the back of her head.

She clapped her hands together as my parents talked to her. "Oh, we have some wonderful dogs here at the moment! I hope you find one that's right for you. We do our best, but they could all use a great family to love them."

I grinned at Deandre. I was sure we would be a great family for any dog!

Miss Hameed led us through a door into a long concrete hallway. On either side of us were big, roomy cages, each with only one dog inside plus a bowl of water, a couple of toys, and a giant pillow or dog bed in the corner.

Most of the dogs rushed to the front of their cages when they heard us come in, and a lot of them started barking.

In the first cage on my left, a German shepherd was lying on his pillow in the back corner. He just blinked at us sadly, like he was too used to disappointment to have any hope anymore. It made my chest hurt looking at his mournful face.

"Maybe we should take him," I said, tugging on my dad's sleeve.

"Miss Hameed says he's quite old," Dad said sympathetically. "He wouldn't be able to play with you very much. But we'll keep him in mind—don't set your heart on the first dog you see, honey."

Another cage held a rotund pit bull mix, who just stood at the door panting at us with her long pink tongue hanging out.

"Aww, she looks like she's smiling," I said, smiling back at her. She wagged her tail at me.

"Her owners gave her up because she wasn't aggressive enough," Miss Hameed said. "Can you imagine? Poor girl. She's a big teddy bear, but nobody wants her because she looks like a pit bull, and they have a terrible reputation."

"*I* want her!" I said.

Dad laughed. "We can't take *all* of them, Michelle."

"She's on a very strict diet right now," Miss Hameed said. She started telling my parents about the diet, but I stopped listening because I saw the dog in the next cage.

He was up on his hind legs with his front paws hooked on the wire mesh. His squashy, floppy face was pressed against the front of the cage like he was trying desperately to see us. When he spotted me, his whole butt started wagging so hard he knocked himself to all fours, and then he started bouncing his front paws up and down. He kept making these sweet whimper-yelp noises like, *Let me out! Please save me! I want to love you SO MUCH!*

"Oh, wow," I said, crouching so our eyes were level with each other. "Hello."

"Ooooorrrrrrrooo," he whimpered, squirming happily.

"That's a boxer," Deandre said from behind me.

"I know," I said, although I'd only been guessing. He was a warm brown color all over except for a swathe of white down his chest and a little stripe of white between his eyes. He had long, slender legs and a sturdy solid body with really short fur. His ears were floppy and his nose was a bit squashed and he had the most enormous sweet brown eyes. There were these adorable wrinkles on his forehead, as if he was *tremendously* worried that I wouldn't like him.

He wasn't small and fluffy like Rosie's dog. He was more like ten times the size of her poodle puppy, Buttons. But his whole face radiated how much he wanted to be loved. I was good at loving things. I was sure I could make him happy.

Behind him in the cage was a strange mess. Bits of white fluff were scattered from one wall to the other next to the remains of disemboweled toys. His dog bed looked like it had been nibbled around the edges. His metal water bowl was upside down in a puddle in the middle of the floor.

Of course, I didn't recognize the warning signs at the time. I didn't even think about them until later. All I noticed right then were the dog's big, hopeful brown eyes.

"He's pretty cool," Deandre said. "I mean . . . that'd be OK with me. If you like him."

The boxer pressed his face against the mesh again, gazing out at me. *Please please please please PLEASE love me*, said his eyes.

"I don't just like him," I said. "I *love* him."

The dog's butt started wagging frantically again, as if he'd understood me. I knew my parents would want me to look at all the other dogs in the shelter before I made up my mind. But it wouldn't make any difference.

I'd found my dog.

Read them all!

Runaway Retriever

Merlin is a great dog.

Parker's new golden retriever is a guy's best friend, with tons of energy for walks and playing catch. And Merlin clearly thinks Parker is the best thing since rawhide bones.

There's just one thing . . .

Merlin is an escape artist. No fence is too high, no cage too strong to keep him from following Parker everywhere he goes. Can Parker make Merlin sit—and *stay*?

Loudest Beagle on the Block

Trumpet is a great dog.

Ella spends all her time inside, practicing her music for the school talent show. But with her new beagle, Trumpet, she's starting to make new friends and see a whole world away from the piano bench.

There's just one thing . . .

Every time Ella starts to sing, Trumpet howls. Loudly. If Ella doesn't lose her canine costar, she doesn't stand a chance at the show—but can tone-deaf Trumpet tone it down?

Mud-Puddle Poodle

Buttons is a great dog.

When she finally gets a dog of her own, Rosie knows it's going to be perfect—unlike everything else in her chaotic house with four crazy brothers.

There's just one thing . . .

Buttons hates her fancy dog pillow, but she loves a good, dirty pile of leaves! Rosie's new pet is her complete opposite. Can she ever learn to to live with this mess of a dog?

Bulldog Won't Budge

Meatball is a great dog.

Eric has always wanted a dog, so when a bulldog named
Meatball is abandoned at his mother's veterinarian office, Eric
is sure it's fate — he can give Meatball a new home!

There's just one thing . . .

Meatball is stubborn. And slow. Eric wants to go to the park
and play fetch, but Meatball likes to lie in the grass and drool.
Is there anything Eric can do to get this bulldog to budge?

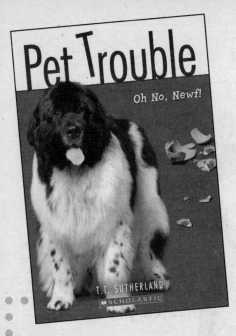

Oh No, Newf!

Yeti is a great dog.

Heidi is dog-crazy. So when she finds a friendly, abandoned Newfoundland, she's determined to take care of him. Even if her parents have forbidden her from bringing a dog home, she'll find a way—by keeping Yeti in her friend's shed!

There's just one thing . . .

Yeti is sweet, and Heidi wants to give him a real home. But he's also enormous and clumsy, and basically her parents' worst nightmare. Can Heidi turn him into a model dog? Or is Yeti just too big to handle?